Echolocation

And Other Stories

Sarah Cimarusti

ISBN: 979-8-218-19480-2

Cover designed by Irene Martinez

Book edited by Ruth Tang

Table of Contents

ECHOLOCATION

J ust to be clear: I wanted to be a dolphin trainer first, not a writer. Though I had suspicions that my compulsory recordings and verbal foam could possibly amount to something, as long as I didn't outpace myself and prematurely call myself Oz.

When you read enough to know what dedicated writing entails, you know that there's much to lose, fear, and drink. It wasn't until recently that I arranged cutout words and snapshots into a chronological collage that began to make sense to me.

In the beginning, there was music.

My father was a tenor who sounded like Rush's Geddy Lee. He was a rooster of a front man, strutting across lit-up stages in unnecessarily tight leather pants. Years later, I'd stumble upon his old high school yearbook and listen to my uncle chortle stories about the women who would swoon for him.

My dad played in garage bands before meeting my mother, an eccentric songwriter who dreamed of being a missionary. She funneled her feelings into music and faith. She fancied my dad enough, but she had her eyeballs on the drummer first.

Everyone experiences love differently. Some people do screwy things under its influence. Eventually, my dad gave her an ultimatum. Marry me, or I'm moving to California without you. They quickly married under a gazebo in the Chicago suburbs.

She wrote songs with my dad while I rolled around in her womb. Everything about her was music. She carried a tambourine in her purse and tied silver bells to the ends of her hair. My parents dreamed of traveling together and making Christian rock music.

Life happened; shit happened. They claimed bankruptcy the year after I was born.

We lived on the third floor of a small apartment in River Grove. I remember a brown, well-loved couch that I would throw myself onto in fits of joy or rage. I see myself dumping a box of Cheerios onto the floor. Shoving a watermelon seed up my nose and begging my grandma to help me pull it out.

I also remember my fourth birthday party, where I cried in the bathroom. I was upset I still had to get my daily shot even though it was my birthday. As a kid, my anxiety was so bad that my body wasn't allowing itself to have regular bowel movements. I couldn't for the life of me take a dump. I'd kick my legs on the toilet while reading the back of shampoo bottles. I don't know why the reading helped me; it just did. There's got to be some scientific reason why.

One of my first memories is dancing around my living room in my diaper like a baby ballerina. My dad wore headphones the size of earmuffs and recorded music on a keyboard. I wrote a poem about it. It goes like this:

A little girl spins
in broken figure eights.

What is this clean diaper,
barefoot freedom?

She dances around
and around on little toes,
pink as a newborn's.

Fantasia's on television
playing the part where
a fish with eyelashes
spins; its tailfin a veil
sheer as curtains.

The fish whirls and blurs
while the girl's father plays
piano in the background.
His fingers patter across
black and white keys.

Keyboard setting:
organs laugh and cry
crescendos that blare
from the stereo.

He rises in one swoop,
scoops her into his arms;
his headphones dangle.
Inside is an ocean of sound
of cymbals, cymbals, cymbals.

She's still spinning in his arms.

I wanted to be my parents before anything else,
even a dolphin trainer. So, I wrote songs and
dabbled in piano, barely mastering the point where
you play a different rhythm on each hand. I
inherited my father's voice and mother's writing
hands.

I had journals upon journals. Dream journals.
Exercise journals. Journals I filled with the names
of shaggy-haired skater boys who thought I was too
loud and wore too much makeup. Yeah, I'm looking
at you, first crush Mike Swanson. He once had his
mom call the police on me for standing outside their
house and watching him skateboard for too long. I

just wanted to feel the torture of unrequited love and watch him do kickflips like a wannabe Tony Hawk.

I dedicated an entire journal to my mother and her deteriorating health. Shortly after she and my father separated, she was diagnosed with multiple sclerosis. She began to introduce herself as the sick single mom with three kids. I wrote about her pain, then drowned myself in *Spongebob Squarepants* re-runs with friends who could relate—with their own dinnertime dysfunction—and escape into fun fiction with me.

We moved from apartment to apartment, but that didn't stop me from recreating HOME. Every one of my rooms was a paper palace. It was like I was living inside a scrapbook. There was a wall I designated for everything. One wall displayed a woman I made out of magazine and newspaper parts. One wall served as a photographic tribute to everyone I had ever known and loved. Another was a wall full of songs I scribbled down on fancy stationery.

6

Every letter that anyone ever wrote me hung from a rainbow-colored string I stuck to the ceiling. I'd fall asleep listening to the fan and soft brush of dangled secrets, half-dreaming underneath my version of stars—stars that read *Hi! You R Awesome.*

In high school, I discovered poetry slams. I met a girl—let's call her Sophie—who threw words like sucker punches. When I listened to Sophie, it was like seeing the same ghosts someone else saw. Her bravery encouraged me to share some work I had hoarded in the paper palace. I was an ornery thing in neon orange Converse. To me, poetry was all about identity and defiance.

I started to choke on my words and fumble with the morality of writing during my early twenties. Studying literature, but also social work, I learned a little about analyzing people's demons, the cagelike systems we all rattle around in, and that there is a real call to serve the human heart and soul. The trouble was, I didn't receive the call to social work. Not even a text.

7

In servitude, you're supposed to have this infamously thick skin—but what happens when people's stories seep into your pores? What if you're moved by the weight and sound of words? Can storytelling be an act of service?

I guess I didn't realize that, in creating my own universe, I'd find people like me. To me it was a survivalist's compulsion. As it turns out, though, words are the visual and sonic breadcrumbs that lead us to others like us.

LOBSTER

One Friday night, Dad thuds through the door, teetering under the weight of two packages. His worn Timberland boots are untied, and for a second it looks like he might Humpty Dumpty his way down.

"Help me with this, will ya guys?" he asks my sister, Lee, and me, elbowing his way through our half-kitchen.

We spring up from the couch, two Power Rangers ready to morph into action. We're both donning long shirts that drape over our knees— Dad's old work shirts that still smell like sawdust and car oil. I pull the box from underneath my dad's chin and set it on top of the counter. I gasp when the box inches forward on its own.

My mother emerges from her cavern. There's a trail of mascara smeared under her left eye.

"Vinni, what did you do?" she asks.

"I got us a raise today, baby!" My mother raises an eyebrow. "Wow, that's great, Vin. How did you pull that off?

"I told Bob I was done. One more repair, and I was walking. Remember I was telling you he was in a tight spot because everyone is quitting on him and going for those fancy union jobs?" Dad explains in his normal speaking voice, one decibel away from a yell.

"Yeah, yeah," Mom rolls her wrists. *Get to the point.*

"Well, get this—I threatened to quit, and he gave me a five-dollar raise. Right on the spot. They don't know how good they've got it. I'm da man!"

"Da man, indeed. So what's all this?" she points at the boxes.

"Oh, this? This is just a little celebration," he says, about to give a demo. "I got us a new stereo since the one we have now is a piece of crap. This one even has one of those outlets that can connect to my recording equipment. And you don't have to mess with the antenna anymore."

10

"Oh…" Mom sighs. "I wish you'd told me first."

"What for? You said you hated the one we have."

"Yeah, but I didn't say buy a new one. We could do other things with that money."

"What about this box?" asks a wide-eyed Lee, jabbing it with her plump finger.

"Well, let's have a look-see, eh?" he says with a wink. "Have you ladies ever tasted fresh Maine lobster? It's your mother's favorite."

"What's lobster?" Lee asks.

"Seafood," I say triumphantly, proud to know an answer.

"Ew, fish," Lee pouts.

"You have to try this. Dip it in some butter, and it just melts in your mouth," Dad says rubbing his hands together.

"Vinni, I wish you would have told me," Mom repeats, but her disappointment is overpowered by a loud clanking in the dishwasher. Dad gives it a swift kick, and it quiets down, resuming the normal wash cycle.

He directs his attention back to the smaller box. He carefully lifts what appears to be a giant spider with two claws. Lee and I shriek.

"Isn't he cute?" Dad picks up a taped-up claw and uses it to talk to my mom. "But Rena, don't you love me?" The lobster's eyes are two black beads on long stalks. I can't tell where they're looking. It's the ugliest thing I've ever seen.

"I taste so good. So juicy. Kiss me, baby," Dad puppets the lobster. "If you don't like me, maybe you'll like one of my friends."

Lee and I stare warily at the box still shuffling on the counter.

Mom glares, but I notice a muscle twitch around her mouth like she's trying really hard not to laugh at our reaction.

The lobster flaps a tail that reminds me of the Chinese fan my grandma gave me. The flapping causes Dad to drop it on the counter.

"Vinni, get that fucking lobster off my counter!"

12

It scurries over to the sink, moving one creepy leg at a time. Its legs clink against the counter's tiles, and Dad scoops it up and shoves it back into its box.

"Nice try, pal," he says.

Mom sighs dramatically and drags her slippered feet across the kitchen. She's wearing her favorite pair of butterfly print pajama pants. It's the first time we've seen her all day since she told us she wasn't feeling well and to "entertain ourselves".

She rummages through the cabinets. Finally, she procures a large silver pot, carries it to the sink, and fills it with water.

Dad has moved on to his second box, ripping styrofoam out of it and tossing it on to the kitchen table. His eyes brim with boyish excitement as he unravels the cord streaming from the back of a large metallic speaker.

"Music and lobster. Now that's what I call a Friday night!" Dad booms.

"Dad?" Lee asks.

13

Dad begins to pile each piece of the stereo system on top of the next. Sunlight bounces back and forth between the volume dial and his glasses. He looks like a mad scientist.

"Dad?" Lee asks again.

"What, Lee?" he demands.

"I'm not eating that thing."

"You're gonna try it. If you don't like it, then don't eat it. You can have leftover Sloppy Joes."

"I don't want Sloppy Joes."

"That's because you're a spoiled little brat."

They engage in one of their signature blue-eyed stare downs. Lee's bottom lip is out, which means a flash flood of tears could arrive at any moment. Dad's lips are pressed tightly together as he swallows the rest of his words.

"The water's boiling!" Mom calls.

"YOU'RE GOING TO BOIL THE LOBSTER?" Lee cries, throwing up her arms. She's had enough.

"That's how you cook it, you goof!" Dad laughs his favorite Bozo the clown impression. He pats Lee on the head and joins Mom in the kitchen.

"Are *you* going to eat it?" she asks me.

"I mean, yeah, what's the big deal?" I say, even though our under the sea dinner makes me shudder.

"It has eight legs, Sarah! Member that furry bug in the bathtub?"

"It's not a bug, though," I say, rolling my eyes.

"It walks like one."

"You're a baby."

"No, you are."

Lee grabs a fistful of my hair and gives it a yank. I wind up, fists aimed at her stomach.

"Don't you even think about it, Sarah!" Mom charges in behind us. "Knock it off, you two!"

"Girls! You wanna hear a lobster scream? Come in here!"

I shove past Lee and bolt into the kitchen. Dad holds the lobster above the bubbling water. It droops in its shell.

15

"Goodbye, lobster," I say, the sadness suddenly filling me. "Dad, is it going to hurt him?"

"Only for a few seconds, sweetie."

Dad plunges it headfirst into the pot. I hear a few clinks, and then nothing.

"I don't hear any screams," I say, relief filling my cheeks.

"Yeah, me neither," says Lee from behind me.

"Wait, what's that noise?" Dad asks.

Lee takes a big gulp of air and holds it. We wait in silence.

"EEEEEEK," Dad squeals in my face. I shove his leg with my whole body.

Mom and I set the table. She folds. I place silverware. As she folds a napkin in half, I can't help but notice the exclamation point she leaves at the end of every place setting. Lobster must really be her favorite.

Dad places a heaping platter on the table. It's layered in garnish, lemon, and four flaming red lobsters. This is followed by salad, corn on the cob, and a swirling pool of butter. Steam rises and swarms the dining room light. Lee, who has been playing Barbies on the arm of the couch, now takes her seat. She grimaces.

"Lee, you don't have to eat the whole thing," Dad says.

We settle into our chairs like royals about to partake in an epic feast. Lee and I invented this game called Polite Ladies; we pretend to be fancy women who order extravagant meals. Lee goes by the name Terese, and I respond to Grace. We ask each other to pass the ketchup in British accents.

Lee and I scrunch up our faces at each other from across the table. Dad pours Mom a glass of white wine. Red makes her sick. Once, my dad carried her up the stairs after a night out, when she overdid the red.

"That's enough, Vinni," she says when he reaches the halfway point.

The three of us watch as Dad carefully positions his lobster between a pair of metal jaws. He clenches them together, and there's a large crack. Bits of shell torpedo the table.

17

"You broked his shell?" Lee asks.

"Yeah sweetie, you have to break through the shell to get to the meat you can eat," Mom says.

"I got yours, Lee," Dad assures her, forking the meat from his and piling it onto his plate.

Mom braves the first taste. She chews her wad of food slowly, letting it roll from one side of her mouth to the other. She closes her eyes. It's the same face she makes when she's taking a bath.

"Good?" Dad leans in across the table in anticipation.

"Oh yes," Mom sighs.

"That's what I like to hear!"

We all dig in. Lee nurses an ear of corn. I prod a piece of silky white meat with my fork.

"Dunk that sucker into some butter," Dad says with his mouth half full.

I plunge the meat into the golden pool. It drips onto my plate. I shove the whole piece into my mouth and get that first hint of butter. It slips across my tongue. It's soft, sweet, smooth.

Dad beams proudly. He munches on his ear of corn, every now and then picking kernels from his smile with a toothpick.

Lee stares him down again. She plucks a corner of her white meat with her fingers. Like it's covered in filth. Her arm shakes violently as she brings it to her lips. She takes a small bite with her front teeth and chews with caution.

"I have to go to the bathroom," she says.

"Take two more bites first," Mom says.

"No, it's disgusting!"

"Fine, then eat the rest of your corn."

"I've lost my apple-tite."

"Then go to your room."

"What for?"

"Lee, go to your room. I can't stand to look at you right now. Some of us actually want to enjoy a meal in peace."

"Lee, listen to your mother," Dad says.

Mom pushes away her plate. I can tell she won't be eating the rest of hers either.

"Vinni, this was too expensive. I wish you would have called me first. I mean, you do this all the time. Show up with shit we don't need when we're behind on things like car payments. The girls don't even like the food," she says, glaring at him.

"I like mine!" I say, shoveling more food into my mouth.

Dad looks like a deflated balloon. He stands up and grabs his car keys off the counter.

"I'll be back later," he says.

"You better be sober."

"Oh, give it a rest for one second of your life, will you, Rena?" He slams the door and the chain rattles against it.

Lee and I pretend to sleep when Mom checks in on us. When the coast is clear we resume our sock puppet performance, a game we play in the shadows cast against the wall between our bunk beds. Sometimes, after our game I'll ask her to sleep in my bunk with me.

We hear Dad stumble through the door. He pounds around the kitchen, opening the fridge and cabinets. There's a clang in the living room, followed by a rustle from the radio, then a man's soothing voice.

It's one of my dad's favorite songs. By this band called Survivor, who he and his old band mates used to cover at local venues full of other sweaty, beer-infused music lovers. His eyes always look extra shiny when he talks about his band days. It's like he's not even in the room with us.

"What's he doing?" Lee asks in a harsh whisper.

"Mom is going to freak."

"Girls!" he calls from the other room. "Girls, come out here!"

Lee pops her head out from the bottom bunk.

"Are you going?" I ask. The thought of my mother in tornado form, peeling around the corner, makes me shiver.

"Are you too chicken?" Lee asks me, now standing at the foot of the bed, her hair nested on the top of her head.

"Nope, let's go," I say, feeling heroic.

"Your breath smells."

"So does yours."

Dad's in the living room pressing into his keyboards now. His eyes are closed. He rocks his body back and forth.

"Dad?" Lee asks like she's poking a sleeping animal awake.

His eyes shoot open and flash blue. The sharp smell of him makes my eyes water. Mom hates this smell.

"My babies!" he jumps up to embrace Lee and me, frozen in our PJs.

"Girls!" He taps a heel on the algae green carpet. "Dance with me!"

I stammer. Lee shoves past me and grabs Dad's extended hand. Lee stands on Dad's boots, and he totters with her on his toes, around and around. They look like a couple of goons.

"Vinni, you better have a good explanation." Mom stomps her foot behind me. I scoot over to the wall and suck in my gut, wishing I was invisible.

Lee and Dad stop in their clown-footed tracks. A high-pitched guitar solo soars through the room.

The chorus picks up again, and Lee says, "Guys, look what I can do." She attempts to show us a dance move, missteps, and wipes out on the floor.

I cave into a fit of laughter. Lee laughs too. It's a snowball of laughter. It melts into the music.

Dad grabs Mom around the waist. She's stiff for a second, but the laughter has softened her. She settles into Dad's grip and shakes her hips. Lee and I smile, embarrassed for them both. They dance forward and back like two lobsters fanning their tails.

NATIVITY

I was baptized on a stage. The floor opened up like the moon going through all its phases at once. I wore a thin white robe over my dad's electrical union t-shirt that hung at my knees. I looked bodiless in the robe, which clung to me like a wet plastic bag.

When Pastor John pushed my head under water, I opened my eyes wide to see my radiant rebirth, but could only make out shadows. I thought about myself as a pair of old pants going through the wash. I was made of grass stains, grease, dried up blots of blood. When I rose to the surface, I'd be the purest I'd ever been.

I wanted something dramatic to happen—for my skin to peel back, feel electricity surge through my fingers and toes. Maybe I'd lose oxygen and get a quick glimpse of God.

Pastor John pulled me to the surface, where I was greeted by applause.

What were they clapping for? They didn't even know that I felt like the exact same girl.

Last summer, at camp, my friends and I played that game where you stand in a dark bathroom and chant "Bloody Mary" in the mirror. She's supposed to appear. At one point, everyone screamed. I did too, except I didn't know why I was screaming. Everyone claimed they'd seen her. And when I said I hadn't seen her, everyone just sort of looked at me. So I stomped off in anger because they were all liars.

It was hard to make out anyone in the crowd because the lights were blinding. Their claps bounced off the walls and filled my head. *Who are these people? Why are there so many people I don't know at my baptism?* I began to feel dizzy.

In the church's bathroom, I stared at my face in the mirror. My face was chalky white. I shivered.

That was the first time I was on my church's stage. Tonight, I will be again, joining my peers for the annual Nativity play.

I'm playing Gabriel, the angel that appears to Mary. I get to tell her that she's going to pop out the world's most important baby, and she will name him Jesus. I do feel kind of bad for Mary. She's only a kid like me. She has to marry Joseph, and she barely even knows him. And then this giant angel busts in and tells her what to do, and she has to believe him and be like, "Okay, no problem."

I ask my mom, "Did Joseph and Mary have sex to make Jesus?"

"No," my mom says.

"Did God and Mary have sex then?"

My mom gives me the same look she gave me when she caught me in my room singing along and rubbing my hips to Christina Aguilera's "Genie in a Bottle." When she asked me what I was doing, I told her: "being sexy". Two weeks later, she confiscated Christina.

26

The virginity thing still kind of hurts my head. So, God put a baby into Mary without sex. I have to be the one to explain this to Mary. That she doesn't need her husband Joseph to help her in the baby-making department, because God will poof Jesus into her womb, and he will be the savior of all mankind. No big deal.

My mom makes my halo out of pipe cleaners. It sits like a glittery nest on my head. As she ties my hair into two French braids, she hums "Joy to the World".

I close my eyes as I feel my mom's fingers graze my scalp, which is grateful for her touch. Then she tugs a little hard.

"Ow!" I cry.

"Oh, don't be a baby," she says.

Yesterday, she spent an entire day in bed. She sat up for cigarette breaks and to eat the peanut butter and jelly sandwich and gulp down the milk I brought her. She asked me to open and close her window. I sat on the edge of her bed and watched her chew her food, swallow a sip of milk, slip one of her pills between her teeth, and swallow another sip of milk.

"You're a beautiful angel," she tells me.

We admire her handiwork in the bathroom mirror. My mom's dark hair bends in the light. She applies her lipstick, dabs it with a paper towel, then reapplies it. She smells like burnt coffee.

"Are you afraid of me, though?" I ask.

"Afraid of you?" My mom raises an eyebrow at me. "Why would I be afraid of you?"

"I don't know. Because everyone seems to be afraid of Gabriel."

"Oh," she laughs. "That's just because angels have a commanding presence. And they are not a common sight to see. They are messengers of God, so when they show up, it has to be pretty important."

We have an antique angel on top of our tree. She belonged to my great grandmother, who passed it along to my grandma, who passed it along to my mom.

The angel has tight, blonde curls on top of her head and a blush red dress. She holds a candlestick in each hand. When the tree's plugged in, her lights flicker on and off. One year I plucked her off our tree and sat on top of her. It felt good. I remember wanting to crush her glass cheeks between my thighs.

We take the long way to church so we can marvel over the blocks with big houses and roofs blanketed in snow and lights. My favorite ones are the dripping icicles. And the colorful orbs. Each one reminds me of a mini-Times Square New Year's Eve ball.

All households have traditions, even if they're formed out of desperation. Like having Christmas dinner at IHOP. The kids love it, and the parents blow out sighs of relief that their kids don't know any better.

In our household, we painted on wooden ornaments. Bells that dripped muddy colors and Santa Claus in every shade of skin. We listened to mix tapes with songs by Bruce Springsteen, Stevie

29

Nicks, and Run D.M.C. We made cookies that came out of tubes we pulled from the freezer and cracked onto the counter. Mom always took enough pain pills to feel well enough on holidays. Her smile was better than anything you could unwrap.

Mom taught us Christmas was a time of giving. One year the local fire department checked our family's name off a list and filled our entire living room with presents. We knew it was the firefighters who had filled our living room, not Santa. We scribbled our handwritten letters of gratitude to the firefighters.

Once, Mom arranged a trip for us to deliver a turkey to a disabled stranger who lived in a cramped trailer. It reminded me of a watered-down scene from that show, *Home Makeover*, where everyone says, "Move that bus!" and there's a brand-new home behind it. I always used to cry when the homeowners cried happy tears at the sight of their new home. This was just a turkey, after all, but the act of kindness was enough to make us all tear up together.

When we pull into a parking spot in the huge church lot, I suddenly feel queasy. My mom flicks her cigarette out the window. She begins to rub my back, her reassurance a waterfall down my spine.

"You're gonna do great. Just do your best," she says. "And if your best isn't good enough, well, fuck 'em."

"Yeah, break a leg," my little brother, Cameron, says with a wry smile.

My sister, Lee, looks out the window at the streetlights, ignoring everyone. She's still upset that she's a year too young to be cast in this play. I told her that when we get home we'll put on our own play, and she can wear my halo. This only held her over for the first half of the day.

I'm wearing a robe again, except this time it's made of a scratchy felt. I try to float down the hallway toward my Sunday school room, but I feel heavy, not holy.

The first person I see as I enter the paper-snowflake covered classroom is Tommy, who's playing Joseph. He's wearing the same kind of felt on his face. It's cut into the shape of a beard. Tommy and I lock eyes for a second and quickly look away. I'm pretty sure he knows that I have a crush on him. My friend Rachel, one of the angels in the chorus, has a big mouth.

I feel a stab of hatred as Mary sits next to my Joseph. Anne is the prettiest girl in this class, so everyone automatically assumed she'd play the divine mother. She accepted the invitation with a sheepish smile. It's hard for me to hate Anne fully, because she's so nice to look at and is actually nice. That, and hating people is supposed to be bad.

"Sarah!" Rachel calls to me from the back of the classroom. Her freckled face is covered in gold glitter, and she's beaming. I run over to her, elated and out of breath.

"You're not going to believe this, but Tommy farted really loudly, then lied and told everyone that Matt did it," she said. She tries to whisper, but her giggles puncture the soft words.

Laughter spills from my lips. We laugh and thrash against the wall and into one another like magnets. This is why Rachel is my friend.

"Okay—places, everyone!" Miss Johnson calls.

I like Miss Johnson even though she smells like mildew and tells the same stories over and over again. Last week she brought me cookies and an ice pack after I burned myself with the hot glue gun she told me not to touch.

Miss Johnson herds us onto the stage, and everyone talks in hurried whispers.

"I forgot my staff!" says one of the shepherds, panicking.

"Garret, it's right here," Miss Johnson says.

If there's not a place in heaven for Miss Johnson, then there's no hope for any of us, I think.

I don't show up until the middle half. I'm pacing back and forth, fanning myself, when Miss Johnson ushers me in front of the lights.

I approach the beautiful Anne and look into her big raindrop eyes.

The lights are suddenly accusatory. I don't belong here, pretending to be one of God's right-hand angels. My cheeks burn, and I forget my lines. Until I feel a gust of wind fill my lungs. I do know the words. The Lord is the word, and he's speaking through me. *Use me, oh Lord*, I plead in my heart.

"Don't be afraid, Mary. You have found favor with God. You will become pregnant, give birth to a son, and name him Jesus," I say loudly into the microphone.

Anne looks at me like she's about to cry. All I want to do is hug her. Her whole life is over. She says, "But how can this be? I'm a virgin!"

"Nothing is impossible with God," I thunder.

Angels come in all forms. They send messages. They whisper joy. They bring death.

I can see my mom in the front row, her face glistening with tears. Her face disappears as the curtain goes down. The crowd cheers while my heart pounds in the dark.

TINY TORNADO

Illinois was a mother state, but Dad made up for it on Saturdays, though he was consistently an hour late. I remember peeling back my room's chipped blinds, the windowpane smudged with greasy fingers.

Finally, I'd watch him pull up in his Toyota Corolla. The silver box had 210,000 miles on it and a back seat baked in dust and sunshine. The second he stepped out, we'd launch ourselves at him as he stood with hairy, open arms in the grass outside our apartment.

Dad always had a full day of fun planned for us.

For a while, riding shotgun was all mine. Until my siblings' heads started cropping up over their seatbelts. Then it was fair game. We were a restless lot, shouting out state capitals and laughing at license plates and bumper stickers that insulted us. Each of us had our own deep gut laugh. Laughter bubbled up in the backs of our throats. We rolled up windows and then rolled them back down again. Our busy, brown hair formed one unapologetic tangle. Music bounced from one end of the car to another, like a beach ball.

Sometimes, there was a loud vibration that streamed from the window and pierced our eardrums. I asked my dad why that happened. He didn't know.

Years later, I learned that it was called Helmholtz resonance, or a rapid pressure oscillation. It happens when the air pressure is higher in the car than it is outside the car. A little bit of air sneaks out again, but quickly rushes in to make up for lost pressure. It sounded like a tiny tornado.

One Saturday, we were on our way to the pool. My sister dangled her swimsuit out the window, and it plopped in the middle of the street. My sister's pink bottom lip blossomed into a full pout. She twiddled her fingers, afraid to tell my dad.

"Wow, nice going," said Cameron.

"You gotta tell him," I told Lee.

"But he's gonna be angry with me," said Lee.

"Don't you want to go swimming, though?"

Finally, Lee regurgitated the confession. "Dad, I dropped my bathing suit out the window!"

Her blue eyes swelled, as if she'd already opened them in over-chlorinated water.

"What, are you stupid?" he asked.

Silence flooded the entire car.

Lee sunk into herself. You could tell she felt stupid. I felt stupid for her. My father swung his arm around the passenger seat and turned to get a view of the traffic behind us and of my shrinking sister. I stared at the gray hair poking out from his ears. He backed his car all the way down a long median.

He exited his car and stood on the median, waiting for cars to pass. Some rubberneckers slowed down, and he swatted them away. Then he barreled into the middle of the left-hand lane, where my sister's swimsuit sat in a heap.

When he bent down to strip her polka-dotted one-piece off the pavement, a car swerved around him, nearly hitting him. The man inside the car waved his fat fists. I swear I could see the meaty blood vessel on my dad's head pulse before he took off after the car, barreling down the street in broad daylight like some kind of Tarzan. We held our breath for what felt like several minutes.

By the time Dad came back to us, he was damp and panting. His eyes flickered wildly, and he grinned. One of his front teeth was always whiter than all the rest—he'd lost the real one trying to catch a fly ball back when he was a kid.

"Who's ready for the pool?" he asked.

That day at the pool, my sister jumped off the diving board and hit the water with so much force, it sounded like her body had cracked in half. We gathered around her and sniffed our pool-loosened snot, while my father rubbed her sunburnt back. He asked her what would make her feel better.

She sniffed. "Oh, I don't know. A Slurpee?"

"All right. Let's get Slurpees then. Everyone back in!" he chirped.

We all piled back into the Corolla, rolling up and down the windows, until our ears could no longer take the pressure.

RICKY LUNA

I t's the end of the school year, and our apartment's air conditioner sputters on and begins to drip. Mom tells us she's landed us a new day camp to attend. My brother and sister are in the middle of a heated argument about how many times my brother has to wash his hands before he's allowed to come into our room. (Twice. And he has to take one shower.)

"Did you hear me?" Mom calls, smoke from her cigarette filling our doorway. "I can't wait to get you guys the hell out of my hair this summer."

We're thrilled with this news. Going to camp sounds much more fun than sitting on the couch for hours, watching the verdict be delivered on *The Maury Povich Show*: who is or who is not the father.

We spring out of bed and slop together peanut butter and jelly sandwiches in no time every morning while she helps herself to an entire pot of coffee. We know better than to start a conversation with her before she finishes her second cup and a full cigarette.

"You guys ready to go or what?" she asks, leaning against a lacquered blue cane and clinging onto a lipstick-stained mug. Her dark waves run wild around her shoulders. She looks like a lady of the night with her smokey eye makeup and thick bangs. My mother is likely the prettiest disabled woman you'll ever see.

Sometimes she watches us play at the public park outside the camp's facility. This is horrifying because she'll bring a portable boom box with her, turn on "Rhiannon" by Fleetwood Mac, and pull out a small silver tambourine from her purse. She shakes it, and the sound of its jingles fills me with jitters.

Lee and I flee to the farthest end of the park and pretend this one-woman show isn't connected to us

41

in any way. Our observant friend Amy catches on, though. "Is that your mom?" she asks us at the swing set. Mom shakes her tambourine at us and smiles.

"I've never seen that crazy lady in my life," I say.

"Sarah, don't lie," Lee scolds me.

So much for being normal in front of our friends.

Finally, it's Cameron who crosses the lava of wood chips to get to her. "Mom, this is really embarrassing. Can you please go home?" he pleads.

Because this is coming from the baby of the family, she takes the news less harshly. But she knows who it's really coming from. Her eyes dart over to me from across the park. "I'm sorry that my children are embarrassed of me," she tells Cameron.

A piercing guilt and wave of relief meet somewhere in the middle of my chest the day she doesn't show up. And the next. We resume our play in peace.

By the end of the summer, I have several friends, and I'm in love with my camp counselor, Ricky Luna, a twenty-five-year-old rock climber who reminds me of my Ken doll and his plastic six-pack.

I climb onto Ricky's back and wrap my legs around him like a primate. He sprints with me on his back past the park and baseball field, then around to the front of the recreation center. Panting, he crouches down, and I slide off his back.

"Okay, kiddo, that was fun, but I think you better go run along and play with your friends," he says in between big breaths.

"Amy is sick today," I pout.

"How about Anna?" he asks. He lifts his t-shirt to wipe the sweat off his forehead. My stomach flutters at the flash of hair around his belly button.

"She's inside playing dodgeball, and I don't want to play dodgeball."

"Okay, what about Lee?"

"I share a bunk bed with her. I see her enough," I explain.

"Well, I got stuff to do, little lady," he says, and, as he places his hand on my shoulder, I hold my breath. "We'll hang out again soon, okay?"

I thrust out my pinkie. He links his with mine. His fingers are large and rough as tree bark, while mine are small and slimy as worms.

As I watch Ricky head back toward the baseball field, I can't help but feel a stab of sadness. I wish I wasn't such a kiddo to him. I don't even have boobs yet, only little stubs. It's such a crime that we don't get to be together.

I find Lee in the art room. She's cutting a circle out of red construction paper, and I slouch down next to her.

"What's the matter with you?" she asks.

"I'm in love with Ricky, and it feels awful," I moan.

"Can you pass the glitter?"

I reach for a small bottle next to my elbow. It's filled with gold flecks. I hand it to Lee.

"You know he's like old enough to be our dad," Lee says, salting her new cutout with glitter.

44

"Uh, what are you talking about? Ricky is only fourteen years older than me."

"He's old enough to be a young dad."

"But not our dad."

"Still. Eww."

"You don't know what you're talking about, Lee. Oh, and by the way, you missed a spot," I say, pointing to a bare patch of red on her creation. Then I stand up and storm out of the room.

Outside the building, two girls sit cross-legged in the grass. One girl braids her friend's golden mane of hair while the other winces and peels open a brown seedpod. A cloud of boys hurls toward me, and I move out of the line of fire.

I scan the grounds for Ricky, but he's nowhere to be found. Today is stupid. It's pretty much over.

I drag my feet toward the park, kicking rocks. My eyes spot a shiny red M&M on the dirty ground. I check to see if anyone's watching me before picking it up, dusting it off and shoving it into my mouth. The sugar dissolves on my tongue. I chew what's left of the shell and watch Tori, another one

45

of our camp counselors, kick her long Gumby legs from the swing set.

Tori has boobs. She can even drive a car. She's really nice to all the kids here. She teaches us how to climb the rope, use a ruler to draw straight lines, and talk about our feelings instead of punching each other in the face. I can't remember wanting to be like anyone more since my half-sister Sammy, who I don't get to see so much anymore since she's been staying with her mom.

I move so close to Tori that I can feel the wind coming off her legs. She swings higher and higher. There's a sheer cloud in the sky that looks like a halo resting on top of her head. Tori pumps her legs and flings herself from her seat on the swing. She glides through the air and lands in the wood chips effortlessly as a cat.

"Whoa!" one kid cries. He and I were the only two people in the park to witness Tori defy gravity.

I can tell by the glassy look in his eyes that he's probably in love with her. Maybe as much as I'm in love with Ricky. Poor guy.

"Miss Tori! Come watch what I can do!" He grabs Tori by the hand.

"Let's see what you do." She flashes him an electric smile. They run off together in the opposite direction.

Tori thinks she's so great, I think, as I sit down on the same swing she sat in moments ago, still warm. I start up the engines in my short legs. I'm smaller than she is, so I can swing higher, probably.

As I begin to climb, all my insides bounce around in my stomach. It's the same feeling I get when I'm around Ricky. Kicking harder and harder, I look up to see if the same halo cloud is over my head, but it's moved. I don't need it.

My mom tells me not to do things other people do for the sake of being cool. Always be yourself and whatever. But as I launch myself out of the swing, I have long Gumby legs and boobs. And Ricky Luna is mine. The wind cradles me and quickly lets go.

47

I pancake onto the ground. There's no air in my lungs. I gasp, too breathless to speak. My arm feels like it's made of Jell-O. The park is one blur of wood chips and shiny red monkey bars. I hear a gaggle of voices coming toward me. I try not to move.

"Sarah, Sarah, hey, are you hurt?" calls a raspy voice. It's the same one that fills my dreams.

The park focuses back into view. I look up at Ricky's face. His caterpillar eyebrows press together when he's worried or mad. One of his hazel eyes has a freckle in it. How have I never noticed this before?

Ricky's genuine concern for me makes me feel more light-headed than I already am. For a quick second, I forget about the throbbing pain pressing into the entire right side of my body.

"Oh boy, this is not good," Ricky says. "Dan! Dan! Call an ambulance."

Dan, the thin and pimply counselor, nods at Ricky and races toward the facility. At least a dozen

48

kids have circled the fence along the park, like hungry seagulls.

"Wait, Dan!" Ricky calls after him. Dan stops and swirls around. "Call Sarah's mom, too!"

Ricky slips his hands underneath me, and my whole body collapses into the pain. His hands clench around my middle, and he begins to hoist me into his arms.

"No, Ricky," I say, my voice crackling.

"Sarah, I'm just gonna move you to a softer spot," he coos.

"Just until the ambulance arrives."

I relive the swing scene in my head. Embarrassment washes over me. It's unbearable.

"No, don't touch me! Please go away," I say, tears streaming down my face.

"Sarah…"

"I said go away! LEAVE ME HERE TO DIE!"

"To die?"

"Goooooo! Pu-lease?" I sob the ugliest sob I can muster.

49

"Okay kiddo, but I'm gonna leave Cameron here to look after you." I didn't realize my brother had slipped into our little situation.

"Hey Sarah, Mom's coming soon." He crouches down next to me, a trail of sweat making the freckles on his face sparkle.

Two men in white uniforms lift me into a bed with wheels. Across the park, I can see my mom pull into the parking lot's only handicapped spot. Ricky rushes over to her. I can't hear what they're saying, but I can see him waving his hands wildly and pointing to the swing set. She says something. He says something. She laughs and shakes her head.

What can possibly be funny right now?

My mom's blue cane hits the ground. All the kids in the entire camp have gathered now. They watch her walk toward us. To me, it's as if she's walking in slow-mo.

"Oh, my poor little girl," she says when she reaches us. I'm surprised at how relieved I am to hear these words.

50

"Can I ride with her?" she asks one of the paramedics.

"Of course, ma'am," he says.

Then she says to Ricky, "Their father is coming to pick up Cameron and Lee."

He nods quietly and smiles at her.

"Feel better soon, kiddo," he tells me before the paramedic shuts the ambulance doors.

The paramedic gives me medicine that makes my head feel fuzzy. My mom holds my hand, petting it gently.

"I brought you something," she says.

"What?" I sniffle.

She reaches into her purse and pulls out a black mass, which turns out to be my stuffed cat, Midnight. Her body flops to one side from years of love.

"I figured you'd probably want her."

"Thanks, Mom."

"I'm so sorry you're hurt, hunny."

"It's okay."

The ambulance jolts, and I brace myself. I glance around, looking at all the wires and equipment on the walls. My mom pets my hand while I cling to Midnight.

After what feels like forever, she says, "Hey, that camp counselor of yours seems pretty nice, huh?"

"Who?" I ask pretending to not know what she's talking about.

"Ricky, he said his name was?"

"Oh, him. Yeah, I guess so," I cough.

Then she laughs to herself like a girl with a secret.

"What's so funny?"

"Nothing, nothing."

"No, what, Mom?"

"Okay, so Ricky asked me out. When all this blows over and you feel better, he said maybe we can go on a date. Right there in the parking lot. I mean it was kind of inappropriate given the timing, you know?"

"What?" is the only word that can possibly escape my mouth.

"Don't worry, I would never date one of your camp counselors, or a teacher for that matter. Plus, he's basically a boy. Handsome, but too young for me. I guess I'm flattered, but no thank you."

This. This is what heartbreak must feel like. I finally know.

PARAKEET

Our family parakeet slipped out the screen door one spring. There was a brief breeze, a sudden flap of yellow, and she was gone. The sky devoured her like she was a slice of pineapple.

For months, her cage hung from the ceiling like a wire grave. She was a suspicious bird, and you couldn't blame her for that. There was a time when I scooped her up, nearly drowning her in a Frisbee of bubbles.

"Birds can give themselves baths!" my mom screamed.

Her little heart throbbed in her chest so ferociously I thought it would stop. I cried from the weight of the guilt and celebrated when she fully recovered from the trauma.

My sister was the overeager petter; my brother, a jack-in-the-box made in hell. She began to lose feathers from all the stress. No wonder she left. And when that fateful door swung open she probably thought, *It's now or never, Chicky. Shake a tail feather!*

All spring, storms raged like teenagers pounding on doors. We ran without rain boots through their puddles and looked up at the sky wondering where she could be. There was no way she could survive the hellish winds. She was too housebroken.

One summer, just around the same time we finally retired her cage, she reappeared. My mother was dyeing her gray roots in the kitchen sink while my sister and I were digging up earthworms in the backyard. I was thinking about peeling one open and counting its hearts. Someone at school told me earthworms had like ten hearts, and I wanted to know if it was true.

"Sarah! Sarah!" Lee screamed. "She's back! Sonny is back!"

I accidentally kicked over a bucket of dirt trying to see where Lee was pointing. A single drop of yellow sat in the middle of the wire fence. My eyes focused—and sure enough, it was her. She bobbled like a bowling pin. Her feathers were all puffed up, and she seemed rather pleased with herself.

"Mom! Look, look!" Lee and I called up to the open third floor window. She popped her face out the window. Her hair was drenched in foam. We pointed at the fence. Mom's eyes widened at the proof of resurrection in our backyard.

She disappeared for several minutes until we watched her run toward the fence with her bath towel stretched out like a fishing net. The bird perched contentedly, her claws hooked around one link in the fence. She didn't budge when the towel fell; she didn't squirm when my mother sealed it shut.

We clung to my mom's heels, anxious to see what the bird would do when she let her loose into our home. The second the towel dropped, she flapped her wings frantically. She collided with the spot on the wall where a cage had once hung.

MARIO IN MELROSE PARK

"You're hilarious, please hang out with me," were the prized first words for my Bumble match.

Not even a month later, Rhett and I order a Coke from the McDonald's drive-thru and ask for a few ketchup packets. Legend has it, their neighbors—Gene & Jude's, home of the famous Chicago-style hotdogs—will kick you out if you ask for ketchup.

When I ask the cashier how her day is going, she rolls her eyes.

"I can't believe you grew up in Melrose Park, but you've never had a Gene and Jude's hotdog," I tease Rhett in a singsong tone.

"You ever have Home Run Pizza?"

"You mean the frozen kind that you throw into the oven?" I ask, tucking my hotdog into my lap and arranging a few napkins to sop up the grease, which is already seeping through the dogs' layers of paper.

"No. I mean the restaurant in Melrose Park that you've clearly never been to."

We're at that stage in dating where we jam connections into various outlets of each other. When it fits, the electricity between us surges. When it doesn't we both get electrocuted. And it turns out we both lived in Melrose Park as kids for roughly two years. Just a few blocks apart.

We could have crossed paths at some point. He could have been a part of the group of boys who liked to set off bottle rockets in the parking lot across the street from me. He could have been eating cotton candy while I was standing in line for the Zipper ride at the carnival that came to town every year.

"Here it is!" Rhett says. "The one with the metal spiral staircase. Just like your dad said."

It was Rhett's idea to eat our hotdogs outside our childhood homes. He showed me the street where his bully beat him up for trying to sell him chocolate, the porch where his grandmother or mother yelled at him to come inside when it got dark.

The homes in this neighborhood crowd against each other, too close for comfort. There are still the clotheslines and rusted chain link fences, the porcelain Mary statues haunting front yards, the asses of air conditioners dripping from second-story windows—just how I remember.

Rhett continues to point at the cramped two-flat. "There's the small yard you were talking about."

I try to place memories in that yard, which is less a yard and more a small strip of brownish grass. The grass where my sister and I challenged each other to cartwheel contests. The patch of dirt I dug worms from to chase my brother with. The small pool that my neighbor Genie cooled her feet in on hot days.

I searched for the fence where my mom had used a bath towel to catch our parakeet.

I know why the caged bird sings, too. Ours finally got a taste of that freedom. So why the hell did she come back?

"This is the one. This was our home," I tell Rhett.

Rhett jerks the car into park and unravels the damp paper from his hotdog. When he takes a bite, he tilts his head back and presses it into the headrest. He smiles at me between the next few bites. His front tooth has a cigarette stain on it. I don't remember the last time I felt this much joy watching another person eat.

"Which floor did you live on?"

"Top."

I stare at the peeling black banister. The first boy I ever loved appears in my memory of the stairs. Biagio, with curls like roots and a voice that always made him sound like he had a cold. The raspy way he'd ask if he could come inside to play Super Mario used to make me feel like I actually could long jump over a pool of lava.

My family was the first on the block to own a Nintendo 64. It was a big deal. We all took turns whipping Bowser into one of the three spiked bombs waiting for us at the end of the Dark World. Even Mom played.

Mario was a plumber, and my Dad was a carpenter and an electrician who helped build the foundation of this small but quaint place. The kitchen had checkerboard tiles and a strawberry pattern my mother had begun to stencil on the walls but had never finished. One Christmas, she came home with a box full of pinecones for us to paint. These were the days we'd work on projects together, with dance music blaring from the radio and light streaming through the blinds and heating up the entire living room.

Mom's health took a nosedive the year I started kindergarten. I was so happy on my first day of school as she helped me button up my black and white dress. I came home with a picture I drew of the coconut tree from *Chicka Chicka Boom Boom*. She put it on the fridge.

Little did I know that, while I was coloring my heart out at school, a phantom pain had overtaken her. No one could figure out what was wrong with her. The doctors prescribed a lot of medications that would make her do odd things. Like the night my dad found her naked in the dark of their bedroom closet, crouched in the corner like a scared cat, murmuring to herself.

My dad could not save her the way Mario saved Princess Peach. He couldn't even save himself. And she'd escape to her friend in Tennessee to cope with his drinking. I will never forget the sight of my dad holding my screaming baby brother by his leg over his crib. How he'd just let go, and my brother would hit the bed face first, the rest of his limbs collapsing all around him in no reasonable order.

Rhett has just polished off his hotdog. "Listen to this song," he says. "Do you hear the bass line? How it walks into the chorus like that?"

"I totally do," I say with more zeal than I intend.

Rhett leans over and plants a greasy kiss on my mouth. My eyes trace the scar on his eyebrow, the single unruly piece of hair that sits on his forehead. I think about how, on the way here, a car nearly rammed into us, and he'd whipped his arm out in front of me to stop me from being launched forward.

Rhett's dad left his family when he was a kid. He says he made peace with it all after he died. Maybe he really has; it's too soon to tell.

I want to tell him about all the things that happened in this house—the good and the bad. I don't know where to begin. I concentrate on the slippery fries waiting to be dunked into ketchup.

That spring in Melrose Park, Illinois, it had rained harder than ever, and the Thirsty Whale bar closed. Dad's snores buzzed under the fan in my parents' stuffy bedroom while Mom, my sister, and I romped around in rain puddles that went up to our waists. Our neighbors frowned and asked why we were playing in dirty water. Mom told them to mind their own goddamn business.

The neighbors couldn't help but be in our business. We were loud about it. Broom bang warnings rang out through the floorboards, but they never compelled us to stop. The police knew us on a first-name basis. They'd roll their eyes and ask: *what is it this time?*

By summer, our throats were ragged, and the rain had dried up. I sat on a lawn chair, bored and alone in our half-backyard, flipping through the water-stained pages of a magazine.

That's when I saw him: a little man with a mustache and red hat with wings, soaring over a castle surrounded by clouds. "Super Mario for Nintendo 64". It was the only thing I cared about at that moment. I didn't have a single cent to my name. I prayed for the game for Christmas so I could save Princess Peach.

A loud crash blasted through the open window on the second floor. The shattering of glass pierced my ears. I left the lawn chair and decided to take a walk—not far, just down the block.

I walked slowly at first, then started to run. I began to rise until my legs skirted the air. I was Mario in a winged cap, weaving in and out of clouds. Circling trees, I was the hero who'd scoop up Mom and carry her far away from Summer '96. I said to myself: swoop down, save all the ones battling Bowsers in their homes.

Somewhere in the distance I heard an echo of a crash, which caused me to falter. The wind wore out my eyes. Rainwater leaked from them. My tiny wings grew weak, and I began to fall. I was not Mario then. I was the sick inside my stomach. I was the air collapsing in my lungs. I was a failure of a daughter falling faster to the ground.

I knew I'd fly as Mario again. Christmas was only a few months away.

ON THE MOVE AGAIN

It takes a few minutes for last night's sleep to leave my eyes and adjust to the light above the stove. It's six a.m. when I reach for the long-corded phone hanging on the wall in the kitchen. The number Mom wants me to call is on the counter. It's written in her bubbly cursive. I cough, clearing the phlegm from my throat.

"Hello, my mom wanted me to ask if you have any boxes that you're not using that we can have," I say to a sleepy-sounding Jewel Osco employee.

"Um, I think that there's a few left over that haven't been broken down yet. I can save them for you, but I can't promise they will be here when my shift is over," he says.

"What's your name?"

"Sarah."

"Alright, Sarah," he says. "I'll tell you what: if you can get here before noon, they're all yours. Ask for Pete."

"Okay, ask for Pete. Are you Pete?

"Yes, I'm Pete. See you before noon, Sarah."

I hang up the phone and waddle back toward my room. I peer into Mom's room. She's sitting upright in her bed, smoking a cigarette. It's still too early for her to be up, but she is a light sleeper and must have heard me in the kitchen.

"Did they have some?" she asks me without turning.

"Yes, they did. We have to be there before noon," I say. She nods.

I head into my room where my sister is snoring on the bottom bunk. Her hair is matted to one side of her face. She has her arms wrapped around her teddy bear, Toby. Toby used to be white but now he's gray and smells like corn chips. Mom tried to wash him once and Lee got really upset, saying she didn't want him to drown.

We haven't even been in this apartment for a year. When Mom told us we were moving again, the bridge of my nose started to burn. I'd just made a friend. Her name is Mara, and she's smart and

67

funny. We both love Pokémon, and we even have matching charm necklaces. She's from the Dominican Republic. Whenever we play by her house, her mom makes us lunches that always have rice and beans in them.

Mom wants to leave this town because it's not safe. A few weeks ago, my brother woke up to a tall shadow outside our home. The shadow was making sharp scratching sounds on the window, and my brother bolted from bed.

"Guys, wake up!" he whispered urgently into our rooms, brandishing a kitchen knife he hid underneath his pillow. We all huddled in my mom's room while she dialed 911.

The police took the man away. Then mom asked Lee and me to drag our mattresses into her bedroom. She wanted all three of us to sleep in her room until she felt we were safe again.

I ask my mom if I can visit our neighbor's koi before we get boxes.

"Bring the walkie talkie," she says.

My neighbor, Beth, has a koi pond. Beth is this old lady who's told me to help myself into her backyard whenever I want. She showed me where she keeps the food for the fish. In a jar right next to her vegetable garden. They know when I'm coming. They swarm together and suck open their mouths for food.

I can spend hours lying on my stomach and watching flashes of silver and orange slice through the water. Beth gave me a book about all the types of fish you can own and how to take care of them. It's hard for me to read and kind of boring, so I don't really read it. But I like the pictures. I dog-eared the page about koi.

Today I find Beth sprinkling her plants with the hose. The sun's in her eyes. She squints in my direction.

"I was wondering if I'd see you today," she says. "The fish are hungry. They've been following me around all morning." Beth always sounds like she's losing her voice. But I've learned that all old people sound like this.

The gate creaks as I lift the lever and join Beth in her backyard. She opens the lid on the food jar, and I drop my hand inside. I throw them into the pond. The fish crisscross in the water, taking turns vacuuming the pellets up.

"I'm moving," I blurt out. "Mom says we have to."

"Oh, well, I'm very sorry to hear it," Beth says. I watch her smile disappear into the wrinkles on her face. "I for one will miss you dearly. You are a good helper and friend. But I'm sure your mom has a very good reason."

"She says it's not safe here."

"Well, your mom is sorta right. This neighborhood is not what it used to be. It sounds like she's thinking about what is best for you kids."

"Yeah, I guess so."

"Hey, don't you worry. You're such a catch, you'll make new friends and settle into your new home in no time."

"I've decided that I don't want to be friends with anyone ever again."

70

"Everyone needs a friend, even if it's just for a little while." Beth winks.

Mom drives us to the store, clutching a mug of coffee that somehow never spills. There's lipstick around the rim. We pass the house with the yellow tape. A few weeks ago, the police busted these guys who were making their own dogs fight for money. My mom rolls down the window and her long waves stream through the crack.

"I have an appointment with my doctor next week," my mom says. "I need you to come with me."

"Okay, but I don't really know what he's saying," I tell her.

"You don't have to know all the medical words. I just need you there as an extra set of ears. And also for support, you know?"

"Okay, Mom."

My mom makes me go with her to her doctor's appointments. She wants me to pay attention because she doesn't trust doctors. Because none of them could figure out why she was always sick. She has this new doctor, though. Dr. Miles, who she met at our church. A few weeks my mom handed me the phone and Dr. Miles told me:

"Your mother has multiple sclerosis. It's a sickness that is hard to see, but it's what makes her lose her balance and really sleepy all the time. It's because she has nerve damage. Do you know what nerves are?"

"No."

"Nerves are your brain's messengers. They tell it to do things. Like run and jump. Well, your mom's nerves are broken. Sometimes they don't send the messages to your mom's brain in time. That's why she falls."

"Is my mom gonna die?" What Dr. Miles tells me scares me. My face swells.

My mom places her arms around my shoulders.

"No, hunny. I could still live a full life," she says softly. Her breath smells like coffee. "But I need you to be a big girl and help Mommy."

Mom and I pull up in front of Jewel. "Thank you, pretty girl," she says, as I shuffle out the door on a quest to find Pete.

SUNFLOWER EYES

Brown Lake was made of fireflies in the summer. There was no need for streetlights, only bugs with lit up butts and jam jars to catch them in. We'd watch them play their love games against glass.

I remember camping in my aunt and uncle's backyard, how much it felt like wilderness. The wet grass underneath the tent. We never packed ourselves in enough layers and shivered through the nights. My dad and uncle used to team up and give us kids a taste of the Scout life. Tractor rides and bonfires. A red toolshed they built with their hands. Pocketknives. Learning to tie knots. Fishing in brown water.

My uncle caught a catfish that swam around in a tank in his basement. He said that the catfish understood him, and when he put his fingers up to the glass, the catfish clapped his flapjack tail toward his fingers. The catfish used to watch us kids argue with, brag to, and dare each other. One night, my pale, redheaded cousin dared me to streak through the backyard. I made him turn around before dropping my clothes and diving into a pool of blackness. The wind stung my skin. This was the first time I remember feeling completely free in my body. I ran around the whole house like an invincible blur. My feet glided through the grass, which stained them with dirt.

My cousin's dare had no power over me. When I rejoined him in the basement, I met a pair of confused eyes that tried to fathom the changed look on my face. I can only imagine that these butterfly effects seemed strange to young boys. The night had birthed me, reinvented me.

The following summer, I'm no longer interested in camping with my dad or truth-or-dare sessions with my siblings and cousins. The neighbor is far more interesting—with his shaggy hair, torn jeans, and oil-stained t-shirts with car logos. He coasts down the street on his bike, slowing down as he

75

passes my cousin's house, pebbles clinging to the wheels. He never looks directly at me.

I use some of my nudist courage to knock on his door. There are cars of various stages of completion parked alongside his house. They lead into his backyard, which is made up of the same wilderness as ours.

A girl roughly the same age as me opens the door. She has eyes like dry ice. A child in her arms has the same eyes. The child sucks on her thumb. She's shirtless, and her cheeks are covered in orange paste. Another kid with frizzy, blonde curls pokes out from behind the girl's leg.

"Is Matt there?" I ask her. The word is new to my lips. I only just learned his name after begging my cousin for it; he'd held it ransom for a few days.

The girl and the kids fixate on me like still rabbits hiding in plain sight.

"Matt, there's someone here to see you," the girl finally calls over her shoulder.

Matt appears in the doorway. It's too dark to tell what shade of green his eyes are. He grabs a set of keys hanging from the wall and joins me outside.

He starts down the street, still not looking at me. I follow and listen to the crunch of gravel underneath our feet. I take quick glances at him and his long, skeletal frame that slouches a little. His hands are in his pockets. He peers downward, kicking rocks.

After what seems like hundreds of steps, I break the silence.

"Did I meet your sister at the door?" I ask. "She seems nice."

"Yeah, sometimes," he says.

"And were those her kids?"

"Yup. My niece and nephew. They have one more sister. About the same age."

The notes in his voice bang into each other. Some seep out low and smooth as smoke, others are high-pitched crackles.

"Oh okay, so how old is your sister?" I ask.

"Eighteen."

For the first time, Matt raises his head and looks at me, scanning my face for judgment. He has the same dry-ice eyes as his family, but his eyes have gold tinsel in them.

I scrape around for more questions, but Matt spares me.

"So, your uncle is a little kooky, huh?"

My muscles clench in defense, but then here is someone who's lived next to my family for his entire short life.

"Yeah, what do you know?" I ask, squinting.

"He talks to himself in the garage late at night— usually about your aunt or the government," Matt explains. "Oh, and sometimes he tells me he's going to cut off my balls."

"Uh, he—what?" I choke on my saliva.

"He's mostly joking," Matt laughs. "I think. Nah, but he's alright. Sometimes I fix his car when it breaks down, and he buys me pizza. We're cool."

"You're cool," I say. I pick at my head as if there's a scab sitting on top of it.

I quake with excitement. He has a dimple on one side of his face. I want to crawl into it and die.

"You sit on the steps a lot." He smiles like he's on to me.

"I like to sit and think," I say. I need him to know I'm an intellectual, not a lovesick girl.

"What do you think about?"

"A lot of things. How summer goes by too fast. How most parents are too wrapped up in their own bullshit. How being an expert at one thing doesn't make you an expert at everything, but no one seems to get that. And anal," I say.

"Huh," he says, chewing on something invisible. "That's a whole lot to think about... wait, did you say anal?"

"Yeah, just seeing if you're paying attention," I laugh. "When you're out late at night on your bike, what do you think about?"

"When I'm riding I like to think about nuthin'," he says.

"Fair enough," I say.

Maybe there's nuthin' left for us to say.

I can hear my aunt's warning about getting too close to Matt and his family. "They're bad news. The parents let their kids roam the streets at all hours and drink beer."

"Oh no, not beer," I told her. Then she grounded me. I'm the only one I know who gets grounded at someone else's house.

Our steps fill the silence. I want to tell Matt about what it's like to run around naked in the dark. The thrill of a breeze between your legs. How every bone and fold of your skin vibrates in celebration. And all of your body parts laugh and recognize one another as family.

"I want to show you something," he says. He grabs my hand, which doesn't know what to do inside his hand. I settle for running my fingers over his fingers' calluses.

Every house on this street is an acre apart. Metal knick-knacks that poke out of yards, plywood, dirt bikes, muddy boats on trailers, spare automobile parts hidden behind sheds with chipped paint. There's not a whole lot to do in this town except collect, tinker, and drive fast on toys that need to be fixed over and over again.

Matt's one of the town's finest tinkerers, from what it sounds like. He is in the middle of restoring his dad's 1970 Dodge Challenger. I imagine him hunched over a greasy engine in a packed garage, a fault line of sweat across his forehead.

"My favorite things to fix and ride are snowmobiles," he tells me, his eyes widening. "There's nothing like a fresh sheet of ice."

The thought of him trekking across frozen water stirs my stomach's acrobats, but I change the subject to our current state of warm air and sunshine.

"So what do you want to show me?" I ask.

"Patience isn't one of your strengths, I can tell," he teases. I sock him in the arm just as hard as I sock my cousin.

"It's just around the lake," he says, as we begin to cross a bridge.

The lake glitters, winking at me. Its waves slosh and give me away.

81

Matt pulls me through the mouth of a trailhead. "We made it," he announces.

I think about us together sitting in lawn chairs, drinking beer, and watching the sun dip down into the horizon. Our shirtless kid drags a wagon full of rocks past my leg. She has my eyes, and she asks me a question. I have an answer for her: this isn't my fantasy.

"Are you okay?" Matt asks me.

"Huh?" My face probably looks as contorted as the scrap of bark I'm staring at.

"Oh, yeah, just thinking," I say.

"Again?" He wags his finger.

The trail wraps around thick woods, streaming with long grass. Floating balls of gnats clog up our faces. We wave them away. One drowns in the corner of my eye. I scrape it out. Matt plucks a long strand of grass and slips it into the side of his mouth.

We see a splotch of white in the distance. The splotch grows as it moves toward us. It grows four legs, a tail. I squeeze Matt's hand.

"Oh, that's just Sandy," Matts says. "His owner lets her roam free during the summer."

Sandy quickly glances in our direction, then breezes past us. The ground shakes under the weight of her. She's a whir of saliva, stench, and nipples, large, drooping nipples. They're shriveled as flat balloons.

"Is she pregnant?" I ask.

"Yeah, most of the time," Matt tells me. "No one really spays around here."

"What a life, popping out babies," I tell Matt.

"Tell me about it," he says. "Okay, we're here."

A large green pathway is separated by two sunflower fields. Golden heads stretch their petals in worship of a blazing sun. The flowers on the left side crane their necks, their shadows cast across the grass where we stand.

Matt flops down onto the grass. I want to float down next to him, but my knees crack loudly, and I wobble onto one shoulder. A corner of my shirt lifts up, exposing a sliver of stomach which my fingers work feverishly to re-cover.

83

Matt and I settle into each other's eyes. His eyes study me. Maybe they've discovered the slight hint of mustache. The chicken pox crater in the middle of my forehead. The battleground of blackheads. Maybe they can trace my birthmarks back to my birth.

"Your eyes are like the center of those sunflowers," Matt tells me.

"My mistress' eyes are nothing like the sun," I recite with a British accent and narrow my eyes.

"What?" he asks.

"Eh, nothing," I laugh, feeling dumb. My cheeks feel like two sunny side up eggs frying in butter. "What were you saying about the sunflowers?"

"Oh, I mean they're creepy but cool," Matt says. "Did you know that the center of a sunflower is hundreds of mini flowers?"

"No, I did not."

I slip this detail into my pocket, to savor for later. I want to share what I know with him, so I circle back, braver this time.

84

"'My mistress' eyes are nothing like the sun,' is a line from a Shakespeare sonnet," I tell him.

"Oh, I never read that one," he says, smoothing the grass between us. "They had us read *Romeo and Juliet* in class. Those two were idiots."

"Yeah, actually, they were a little bit," I laugh.

"I had to drop that class, though. That term my mom got really sick and my older brothers and I had to pitch in to earn some extra cash around the neighborhood to help pay for her medical bills," Matt explains. "I missed a lot of school. The school was pissed. Kept calling the house and threatening everyone."

"Wow," I say, leaning closer until our elbows almost touch. "What happened? Is your mom okay?"

"She's still sick, but she's on medication. My dad got a better job with better insurance and stuff," Matt says. "It was tight for a while, but we manage, like always. We take care of each other."

Matt barely makes it to the end of his sentence before I kiss him hard on the mouth. His lips

85

recognize the motion and melt into mine. He tastes like salt and smells like metal. He presses his body against mine, which absorbs every touch. It makes thousands of photocopies of every imprint, movement. We roll around in the grass between the rows of ten-foot sunflowers that are too focused on their beloved ball of fire to notice the commotion happening underneath them.

My hands act like they've done this hundreds of times before. They reach for his belt, and the leather slithers through them.

He smiles, and there's the dimple again. I want to stick my tongue into it.

Then he says, "Wait."

I'm not sure what this means, but I can feel electricity surging through my fingers, between my legs. My mouth burns and all my follicles are on fire. I fumble with his pants.

Matt grabs my wrists and says calmly, "I just think we should wait. Is that okay?"

I sit up straight in the grass. "Yeah, that's totally fine," I say, shriveling up inside. I can't look at him, so I stare at the sunflowers. The centers of each of them are crowded, black, hideous pits.

"Sarah," he says. I realize this is the first time he has said my name, and I hate him for using it.

"What?" I demand.

"I really like you," he says.

"Could have fooled me."

"I do. A lot. I think we should hang out again." He tugs on a wayward piece of my hair.

I'm unsure of the protocol. In the story of boy meets girl, this doesn't happen. After a while I spit out, "Fine. Let's hang out again."

There are no lights leading the way back to Matt's house. The gravel bounces around under our feet. We hold hands, but neither of us have words.

A light flickers on. The light is the size of a fingernail. Another light flutters on. And another. Thousands of miniscule lanterns appear and disappear. The strange dance fills our silence.

HOME ON FIRE

It's Halloween, and my mom thinks someone is playing tricks on her.

"Where is it? They stole it from me. I just know it," Mom says, rifling through our car. She throws all four doors open. Cameron, Lee, and I stare out the car windows and watch the princesses and superheroes with their mommies and daddies and mouths full of candy.

"They stole it. I can't believe they did this to me," Mom says.

"What's she looking for?" Cameron whispers in my ear and jabs a finger into my ribs.

"I don't know," I tell him. "And don't poke me."

"I'm not sorry," he jeers like a jack-o-lantern.

"Guys, stop talking," Lee says. She crosses her arms tight across her chest and hides behind overgrown bangs. She doesn't want anyone to see

88

us. I agree with Lee. I would much rather pretend we don't exist. But I get out of the car instead.

My mother's knees crack when she bends down and crouches over a suitcase she'd gutted into the street. She's wearing a ruffled sundress. Her hair, neatly pinned back earlier today, flails violently with every fling of her thin wrists. Beads of sweat lick the lines that have been worn into permanent creases on her forehead. Her face reminds me of a piece of paper that has been folded so many times you can split it down the middle.

She tears through checkered underwear, shirts, a blow dryer, and a cell phone charger. She's mumbling aloud to herself and doesn't hear me when I call her. She looks lost in the hazy summer heat, but then she focuses on my face. She lights a cigarette, and her fingers rattle. Her cheeks cave whenever she takes a puff.

"They stole my medicine," she says, blowing out smoke.

"Who stole your medicine?" I ask her calmly.

"Bob and Stella," she says, and grits her teeth.

89

I have seen her like this many times before, so I select my words with precision.

"Mom… I'm not saying I don't believe you. But are you sure? Why would Bob and Stella take your medicine?" I say, placing my hand on her back. She shakes it off.

"Sarah, you don't get it. I need my medicine," she pleads.

"Did you check the trunk?"

"Why don't you help me instead of just sitting your ass there and go check the trunk?" she says, panting.

Bob and Stella, the pastor and wife from our church, took us in after the fire. For a few weeks, they let my brother, sister, mother, and me sleep in their living room on their couch with a built-in bed.

The fire was rampant, one of Southern California's largest. And it was an accident. A hunter lost in the woods set off his flare gun, and the flames spread. It encroached on beautiful homes, hidden in the clouds, on jagged landscapes covered in sunflowers and cacti. It left thousands of stragglers seeking shelter and knocking on family and friends' doors. We had neither. So we turned to the church.

"Never trust anyone, I tell you. Even so-called God people, Sarah. They're all liars," Mom always said.

She leans against her car and begins to suck deeply into her chest, then back out with enough air to fill a balloon before caving into a fit of tears.

I feel embarrassed for her. Guilt drips down my spine as I remember her late last night. She woke up choking. I ran to her in the darkness of her room, asking her what was wrong. She told me she felt electric shocks in her legs and fingers, so I held her close to my chest.

Sometimes my mother's flare-ups are unavoidable. They can happen anywhere at any moment. She once went into a long, eerie trance in the middle of a mall swarming with people. After what felt like several minutes of my siblings and I shaking her shoulders and calling her name, she doubled over and began to sob.

"What's wrong with your mom?" a woman asked me.

"She'll be fine," I snarled.

On days lower on the pain scale, all she wants to do is reunite with her long-lost sun.

"Let's go to the zoo!" she said one bright day.

Lee, Cameron, and I exchanged reluctant glances, but weren't about to snuff the sound of fun. We loaded up the trunk with a cooler containing Mom's medicine and a cold pack in case it was hot. Heat always threw off her balance.

At the zoo, she leaned on her cane and snapped pictures of us in front of a polar bear batting a giant beach ball with an enormous paw. Lee and I linked our arms and wriggled with delight. Cameron flopped around like a seal. Mom captured the smiles on our faces.

"How come the ball doesn't pop?" Cameron screamed, and leaned over the fence.

"Cameron, don't hang on that, please. I don't want you to fall," Mom said.

She looked so happy that day. When people passed us, they peered at her and her cane. They looked at her like she was another animal romping around in an exhibit. It's like they were searching around for a sign filled with facts on my mother's diet, species, origin, and habits in nature.

I didn't like the kind of attention my mother drew. Whether it was judgment or curiosity, I challenged everyone the same way. *Back off*, my eyes barked, like I was a Chihuahua hiding in Mom's purse.

There are days that she lies in bed from morning to night. She barely goes to the bathroom and forgets to eat. I wonder if it's the electric shocks, the fatigue or the nausea, or something else. Maybe she just doesn't want to get out of bed. Maybe she sees no point in it. *Isn't that a sickness too?*

Sometimes, she puts my stubby finger on points hidden under her skin. "There, Sarah. Can you feel that? That little crunchy thing rolling around in there?" I scrunch my eyes up and try my hardest to feel.

Pain has always haunted my mother. She was born from it, and it followed her. It lived in her house, it ate dinner with her, and it was always confusing. Before it was her own body hurting her, it was other people. She has told me stories I have sworn not to tell. They have become my stories too. Her pain has become a part of my own memory. I open the door and join her in the darkness, even though I don't want to because it scares me. And even though she can't see me in the dark.

"Mom, what's going on? Can we go now?" Cameron asks, and Lee cranes her neck. We all want this to be over.

"No, we can't go until I've got my medicine!" she yells.

"Where's your medicine?" Cameron asks.

"In Bob and Stella's house. I'm going to get it," she says.

"Wait, what?" I ask. "Mom, the lights are off. No one's even home."

"Are you going to help me or not?" Mom asks me.

94

I spin around to see if trick-or-treaters are watching us. The blissful frolicking on this street has died down.

"What's going on?" Lee suddenly demands, emerging from the car. She doesn't like to be the only one left out.

"Mom and I are going to get her medicine from Bob and Stella's house," I say. "Just wait here with Cameron."

"Hey, I wanna go too," Cameron whines.

"Lee, can you please stay with Cameron?" I plead.

"Fine. Cameron, do you want to see if we can get some candy?" Lee asks.

"No, I want to go with Sarah and Mom."

"Cameron, *no*. Stay. Right. Here," Mom says, and we're all quiet.

Mom floats toward the house, like something invisible is stringing her along. Her dress ripples in the wind. I follow. I wince with every step I take. I'm wearing a pair of shoes that aren't mine. It's

95

been weeks since I've worn anything that fits me right, that's truly mine.

Mom stares at the front door, like she's willing it to open. She grabs the knob and turns it slowly. Then she raises her arms above her head and pulls a loosened bobby pin from her hair. She inserts it into the door's lock and begins to jiggle it.

"Mom, I don't know about this."

"Sarah, do you know what can happen to me if I don't take my medicine? I can have a seizure, go into a coma, and die. Do you want that?"

"No. Okay, what do you need me to do?"

"Go around the back and check to see if any of the windows and doors are open."

I cross the freshly mowed lawn to the side of the large salmon-colored brick house. It looks sturdy. A fire could take this one down too.

It was three in the morning when my neighbor pounded on our door. Her wide, sapphire eyes ripped me from my half-awake state.

"Summer, what's wrong?" I asked.

"There's a fire! Tell your family everyone needs to leave," she said. As she spoke, orange flames flickered behind her head, dipping in and out of mountains in the far distance.

Summer and I had only known each other for a few months, but she was the best friend I had since moving to Ramona, California. It felt like we just started telling each other secrets. I grabbed Summer's weathered hoodie and hugged her tight. This was our silent goodbye, just in case.

I closed the door behind Summer. The air in my mouth was dry enough to catch fire in the back of my throat. I collected my nerves, cleared the area for words. "Mom, wake up. We have to go."

Cameron and Lee popped their heads out from their rooms, rubbing their eyes and shedding their lingering dreams.

"There's a fire," I told them.

The words felt foreign on my lips. A false alarm resounding in my ears. I felt like I was the prankster yelling "fire, run for your life" on an airplane or in a movie theater. Except I didn't yell it; I simply stated it without any emotion.

We all refused to believe we weren't coming back. Cameron was the first to make sense. He insisted we take the parakeets, which were twittering in their cages.

"I don't want to come back to them barbecued alive!" he yelled. "Are you guys crazy?"

My mother rummaged through the house and grabbed the essentials—medical records, social security cards, and a locked, fireproof box filled with I don't know what.

We helped her heave her cane, walker, wheelchair, and electric scooter into a choking trunk. Of the four items, she only used her cane regularly, but she was always prepared for the future when she would wither away. These things collected dust for now, but stood as chronological reminders of our mother's frailty and impending demise. I hated that these things took up the most space in our four-door maroon death trap with no air conditioner.

Lee took Toby, and I, too, cradled Midnight. Lee jutted out her bottom lip like she had when she was little. She began to cry. I squeezed her shoulder.

I stripped the collage of pictures taped to my wall. One clean sheet of faces of every person I had ever known. I rolled them up tight and sealed their tube with a ponytail holder.

We packed up our car and left in our most practical clothes. I was still wearing my slippers when we rolled away.

We drove in silence and watched bright streaks light up the sky. Flaming wings covered green chunks of earth. When the fire was done with its pillaging, everything would be powder. The winding road to our house would become a graveyard of skeleton trees, blooming with blackness.

I stare at the thick bricks that hold Bob and Stella's house together. I think about this construction site I used to sneak into when I was younger. A few guys wearing bandanas and sawdusted power belts listened to the Stones while stacking wood during the day. I waited until they left, and I sat on a wooden platform where the roof would eventually be. I marveled at the rooms in their infant stages, the craftsmen's handiwork after hours of nurturing. They began with roots.

On the wooden plank, I watched the stars. Every day I visited, the house was bigger, closer to completion. Just a couple of guys. It took them several months to build the structure. And in minutes, if something massive and destructive were to collide with it, it would be rubble. What people make is nothing compared to what the universe can create and take away. The fire snapped its fingers. Then it huffed, puffed, and blew our house down.

I press my nose into Bob and Stella's windows. My breath steams up the view of their furnishings, their decorative couch pillows, coat hooks, flower vases, table placemats, books protruding like teeth in a grin, smiling faces in frames on a mantelpiece. A fireplace. A fireplace to build a toasty fire when the family is cold. I try to lift up a window. Locked.

I think back to our move to California. Dad was with us then, before Mom kicked him out again, and he went back home to Illinois. It had been a perfect day.

We are on our way to California. Yeah, kind of like that song. "Going to California."

Someone told me there's a girl out there... la la la. You know how it goes. Yeah, that's the one.

We're driving to Southern California, trailing behind Dad, winding, hugging the mountains close. The windows open their mouths wide to let loose our outstretched hands that wag like tongues.

I can almost taste the sunshine. Every now and then, I get a whiff of animal dung from the Wild Animal Park.

Mom says there's an ostrich farm close by, and I want to see an egg. "Big as your head," Cameron says. My arm sticks to Lee's. I'm nested between them both.

Mom plays her Pat Benatar tape. *"Heartache through heartache we stand, no promises..."*

101

"Everyone shut the fuck up," she says. "There's no railings."

She's right. There's nothing stopping this car from flying off a cliff right now.

"We are strong," Pat reassures us.

Mom white-knuckles the steering wheel.

"She's totally losing it right now," Cameron snickers.

"Don't fucking talk; I need to concentrate," she says.

Pat rings in my ear. Mom sings along in off-key notes that ricochet around the car. I watch her eyes bat open and closed in the rear-view mirror. I'm clutching the treble clef bars, praying I don't go overboard.

The mountains have rugged backs and sharpened teeth to devour us. These beasts are beautiful, and they know it. The sun knows, too. It warms the mountains' faces.

Cameron pinches me back to life. "Are we almost there?" he asks, sleep leaving his eyes.

"What will our new home be like?" Lee asks.

It's the end of Side One of the cassette. Mom turns Pat to Side Two.

The sun ducks in and out of clouds, weaving in and out of perky peaks. We wind higher, and my ears pop. I shake my head until the sound returns.

"We're going higher, guys," I say. I feel safe and wedged between my brother and sister.

We're going to California. *La la la.*

"Sarah!"

I swivel around in the grass, and my brother peers up at me.

"Cameron? I thought I told you to stay with Lee! Do you ever listen?"

"Jeez, be quiet for a minute. Bob and Stella are in the driveway."

"What?"

"Yeah, they're not happy. They caught Mom."

"Oh shit." We peel across the lawn.

"Go inside, kids," We hear Stella say to her two daughters. They trot past us, their brown ponytails whipping back and forth. They're both wearing matching flowery, high-collared Sunday school dresses. Their arms are heavy with fat bags of candy.

"Rena, I can't believe my eyes," Stella says to Mom. "You're breaking into our house?"

Stella, a nurse, wears the same petite frame as my mother, but she stands with her shoulders back and radiates confidence from her abdomen. Her husband, Bob, stands as still as a gargoyle next to her. His eyes are tired.

"Yes, you stole my medicine," Mom says with a snarl, about to spit.

"Why on earth would we steal your medicine?" Stella asks.

"I don't know, but you stole it. Even though you know how sick I am. Some friend. And you call yourself a Christian."

"I'm sorry," she says. "But the girls and I should be heading to bed now."

"I don't buy it," says Mom. "I looked everywhere. There is no other explanation."

"Your medicine isn't here," she says, angrier this time. "And forgive me, but you didn't look so sick the other day, Rena, when you were on top of your daughter."

"Don't you dare tell me how to parent my kids."

I'd been on Bob and Stella's home phone, calling my boyfriend, Matt, back home in Illinois. It was a dollar per minute to call long distance, and I yammered away for an hour before my mom noticed. I didn't care. I needed to talk to someone who wasn't my family and was a little more human than Bob, Stella, and their ethereal cabbage patch kids. My boyfriend wasn't much help either.

"Sarah!" my mom screamed.

"What?"

"Get off the fucking phone!"

I reacted too slowly for my mother, who catapulted onto me like a graceful lioness. There was no sound. She straddled me in liquid seconds, throwing her delicate fists into my face. Clean and beautiful blows. She hardly weighed a thing. She wrenched the phone from my hands and slapped the hard plastic across my skin. It stung.

I was stronger than she was, but I submitted to her. I let her feel like she was more in control because she'd lost so much of it. I watched the anger settle in a pocket on her forehead.

I glowered at her, letting the hate rise from my gut and fill my face.

"Get off her, Mom!" Lee yelled.

Everyone was confused when I began laughing as Stella walked in on the scene happening in her living room. I wanted to play it off like we were just roughhousing. Just a couple of house cats. The truth was too embarrassing.

Stella's lip was trembling in shock—or maybe disgust. "Rena, I'm sorry, but you and your family need to leave," she had said. "I will not tolerate violence in my home. I have my own kids to think about. They should feel safe."

Stella's lip is trembling again as she remains firmly planted on her lawn, a guardian of all that's green.

Lee, Cameron, and I stare up at the sky, our feet, at the side of the house.

"Please leave, Rena. Or I'm calling the police," she says.

Mom is silent. She sinks into the pool of pastel pink in her dress. She's so small.

Something inside me jerks to attention. It hits Lee and Cameron too. Lee inches closer to my mother. Cameron reaches over and grabs her hand. My mother's army. We're arranged and standing at attention like toy soldiers.

"Come on, kids," Mom says to us. "Let's go home. Wherever that is," she says, and we disassemble.

Cameron finds my mother's medicine in one of the overturned suitcases we lift from the dirt while cleaning up and repacking the car. For the first time that day, my mother smiles.

"Cameron, my good boy," she says, and he beams like a beaver. She lifts her shirt, revealing dark bruises. Her stomach is a map, and the bruises are the mountains, burned by a rampant, fiery illness. She injects herself where the fleshy land is fresh and bare. No black.

On the drive to nowhere, we play license plate games. Mom is listening to her Pat Benatar cassette tape. She smiles at me in the rearview mirror, her brown eyes on mine.

LENNY

I am a mediocre ventriloquist.

I move my mouth to speak on behalf of my backpack, Lenny, a stuffed pink snail with two long stalks balancing eyes the size of pool balls. We travel long school hallways together. One word to describe us: inseparable. When I leave him in my locker, I worry about him being alone in the dark that reeks of rust. So he's with me most of the time.

I don't have a packaged explanation for how he became my best friend. Like most substantial relationships, it was just meant to be. My friends purchased Lenny for me before I moved away to California with my mom and two siblings. At thirteen, I was perhaps a little too old to start fussing around with an inanimate friend, but for the most part Lenny was well received and my sanity left unquestioned.

Lenny has a zipper and a pouch that drops deep into his cushioned shell. But it's important to remember he's so much more than storage for my makeup, cigarettes, and house keys.

He's also a secret keeper. Lenny is with me whenever I decide to ditch first period and sit on a stump in the woods behind my school. Lenny hates the smell of smoke, and I always apologize profusely for subjecting him to such a smelly habit. But I explain to Lenny that the alone time really calms my nerves. Lenny understands this.

Lenny was with me last year, when this kid Zach and I snuck away during a spirit building assembly to fuck in the hallway leading to the pool, which was being renovated my entire sophomore year. I wore a skirt, so I only had to peel off my underwear, which I then stuffed into Lenny. Zach lay on the tile floor with his back pressed against a wall. I was worried about his ass getting too cold, but he said he was fine as he hoisted me on top of him, and I began to bounce up and down. I had rested Lenny on the ground. I noticed how his eyestalks drooped more than usual.

When people ask me questions, I first consult Lenny. Of the two of us, Lenny is the whiz kid. I have told him he is a borderline genius. At this, Lenny usually gives me a blank stare. I can't tell if he knows he is really smart or not. I have a feeling he doesn't know, even though I compliment his intellect all the time.

Whenever my teachers call on me for answers, I will tilt my ear and say, "What's that you say, Lenny?" and sure enough, Lenny will know. A few teachers have prohibited me from speaking on Lenny's behalf in class. They find Lenny inappropriate and distracting. There are others who find my usage of Lenny "creative" and refer to him as a separate entity like most of my classmates and I do.

I have come to realize that most of my fellow classmates are in constant need of good jokes and reassurance. Luckily, Lenny brings both.

We have this vending machine with little slots in the hallway adjacent to the cafeteria. I get a bagel and cream cheese from the machine some mornings. Lenny came up with an idea that I should swap out the bagel with something of my own. I rifled through Lenny and my fingers stumbled upon a tampon.

I could hardly contain myself. Lenny and I were choking on our tongues as we rounded the corner, hearing the responses of amusement, awe, and disdain behind us. One of the school's security guards pounded down the hallway, keys banging against her thigh, and fished $1.50 out of her own wallet to get rid of the obscenity.

This year Lenny and I have decided to do a routine for the school's variety show. Lenny is working hard on his part, providing most of the inspiration and setups. We've been going straight to Ed's apartment to work.

Ed is this middle-aged man who lives alone and has the largest movie collection I've ever seen. He lets me come over whenever I want to watch his movies and eat his food. I'm usually there when he's at work. Sometimes, Lenny and I will ditch first period and chill out on Ed's couch and eat pop tarts. Ed is lonely, but he's never tried anything funny, though once we slept in a bed together. We recited all the lines to Dumb and Dumber until we both trailed off.

Anyway, so Lenny and I have been working on our material, though sometimes we can't help but break character. We roll around on the carpet in agony whenever one of us comes up with a real kicker. A few times, I confess to Lenny that I'm a little afraid to go on stage in front of people. Lenny bashes me on the hand with one of his eyes, and says that we've come too far not to be brave lunatics. I hug Lenny tight.

Two days before the big show, Lenny goes missing. I tear apart my room, dumping my dirty laundry onto the floor, ravaging my drawers. I barrel into my mother's room. She's sitting on her made-up bed and smoking a cigarette. I ask her if

113

she's seen Lenny. She calmly says she gave him away to the Salvation Army, then blows out smoke.

Tears sting my eyes as I demand to know why. She tells me she's worried about me. I don't know what to do, so I pick up a candle from her nightstand and throw it against the wall. I flee. I hear her screaming after me, but before I can make out the words, I'm outside.

I sprint to the Salvation Army a few blocks away from our apartment complex. The door to the facility is no longer automatic; its tired mechanics drag and grind as I push it open with my shoulder. Musty air fills my nose, and I panic, thinking about what a treasure Lenny is, how googly-eyed and adorable he is, and how it may be too late. I have the urge to scream his name, but know how that may come off to people who don't have a context. I search the shelves lined with chipped knick-knacks for my best friend.

A man pushing his mop down an aisle calls out "Closed, folks, fifteen minutes!" so suddenly he almost barks it. It startles everyone standing around him. A woman fumbles with a drawer she was pulling from a jewelry box, and it falls to the floor. She sighs with relief when she realizes it didn't break.

I shuffle through all the spots I already checked once. I feel so fragile and small without Lenny. I keep remembering the naked spot on my back. I wish I were dreaming that I was naked instead. A reality without Lenny surpasses nightmares. How will I amount to anything without him coaching me through? He's so much a part of me, he could be my hippocampus. He stores everything. He's also the weapon I brandish on a daily basis. All the things that I don't like bounce right off that shell of his. Together, we dodge the world.

"Five minutes!" The man with the mop yells these words. He slaps the mop to the floor in sharp, deliberate movements. His head is down, and his shoulders are scrunched tight to his body. If I were to guess, he's holding it together like the rest of us.

I give up. I pick up a neon orange fanny pack with a grease stain that's dangling from a rack and snap it around my waist. What I need is a hat, I think, and sure enough there's a golf hat, green as AstroTurf. Wait. I need . . . beads. I saunter on over to the dusty glass counter and twiddle through the costume jewelry. The one with white marble beads the size of coal, with spiral seashells in between each bead, calls to me. Its clasps seem complicated. And the shells jut out like little daggers. I drape the heavy string around my neck. I put my arms on my waist and survey myself in a body mirror. I'm a demented queen, I conclude.

The woman who was messing with the jewelry box passes behind me and does a double take. I catch her gaze, and she quickly looks away, her short bob snapping to the tune of her neck.

I turn around and face her, completely decked out in my temporary ware. She's standing in line now, trying hard not to look at me. I suddenly want to challenge her. I want to ask her why everyone is so fucking afraid of each other. I want to ask her why we have these neat little roles, when we're all messy and tangled. But most of all I want to ask her name and fling it back at her like I've always known her.

"Hey, kid, we're closing," says the man with the mop, who is now pushing a shopping cart filled to the brim with odds and ends. "And if you want what you're wearing, you're gonna have to get in line now."

I shriek. Inside the cart the man is pushing there's what appears to be an eyeball poking out at me.

"Lenny, is that you?" I suddenly plunge my arms into the cart. I'm a machine left to my own devices, craning toward the prize I will win the first time my hands touch it and grab hold.

"Uh, what?" asks the man, who looks around the store as if to call for a co-worker or help of any kind.

"I want to purchase this," I say, and smile like a two-year-old who's just took a dump in the toilet for the first time. I can feel Lenny snickering into my hands. He probably finds the whole situation hilarious. I give one of his eyes a squeeze, then stroke the side of his shell.

I feel like I owe the man an explanation. "This belongs to me. It's hard to explain, but it's one of my most important things."

"Just take it then. It's yours. But you have to leave now."

I look into the man's eyes. They are foggy and desperate to shut. His long black hair hangs on his face, which is covered in acne scars, scars of his youth.

"Thank you," I tell him.

Lenny and I go back to work at Ed's place. We practice for a little bit, but are more interested in just staring at one another and being silent together. We want to say things but don't have to. We stay up late watching cartoons. I open up Lenny's pouch. My mother had removed all his contents and left them on the kitchen table. He's shrunken, emptier. I rest my head on Lenny as we hunker down.

It's opening night. Lenny and I beef each other up backstage before the opening act. I slap Lenny in the face, and he slaps me back. I pluck a stray thread stuck to the bottom of his shell, and he checks my breath ("stank-free").

Our routine starts off bumpy. I choke on my saliva under the blazing stage lights within the first thirty seconds. Lenny saves the day by calling attention to it, asking me why I insisted on the last shot of bourbon backstage. Then we slide right into our bit. We take on the persona of Holden Caulfield, receiving a few knowing nods from fellow students in the crowd.

We capitalize off our third-period English class, using especially wide-open classmates as inspiration and calling them all old phonies. It's pure roast material that gets some chuckles. This is followed by a moderated burping contest. Lenny and I are neck-and-neck, but he makes it all the way to the letter V. We hand each other ribbons for our success. He gets a gold one, and I get blue. Farts and burps never fail to entertain.

Like I said, I'm not too gifted at ventriloquism; I'm actually the opposite. I widen my eyes.

Enunciate my words. Open my mouth to reveal expansive gums and gaps between most of my teeth. Lenny doesn't even have a mouth, yet for some reason everyone can hear him loud and clear. He rattles off pure filth.

Then we go to our special place; we slip into our high. Lenny and I tell stories on stage like we're alone in my room–the only audience is my magazine collage of defamed celebrities on my wall. Eminem decked out with pink hair and a Hello Kitty tattoo. Amy Lee wearing a crown of thorns. The audience is not my peers. They are not my friends, competitors, enemies, or a mix of all three. They are the rustling of blinds, wind pouring in through my bedroom window. They know everything and nothing about me.

Every now and then I can hear a laugh from the crowd that's rockier, louder, fuller than the rest. It's not a laugh at a punchline; it's my mother screaming my name from the other room. It's me laughing while climbing out the window and thinking of her face when she realizes I'm gone. I have a laugh track always playing inside my head alongside my plan to get out alive.

I signed everyone's yearbook the same. I wrote, "I will remember you in my heart and in my pants." Then I scribbled a drawing of Lenny as my signature.

I went to college. The students had me pegged. The teachers knew what I was all about. No one was amused—they waited patiently for me to step aside or take myself seriously. I met a girl who had escaped a war-felled country. She came to the U.S. desperate, washed ashore with her entire family. She wrote beautifully; little symphonies. I met a guy who lived in a car whose poetry sawed me in half. A professor who had tended the sick and dying alongside Mother Teresa.

I had an internship where I tutored elementary school kids whose parents had signed them over to the state. We watched movies with happy endings, learned about presidents, checked the butterflies in their cocoons, made farting sounds. These activities were punctuated by crisis intervention: one adult putting their body on top of a flailing child's so that the child wouldn't hurt anyone. There was nothing funny about restraining a child who has already lost everything. When angry little bodies went limp underneath my weight, I didn't feel like I'd won anything. It's amazing how allowing myself to be touched by other people's pain dulled my own.

I stopped bringing Lenny everywhere I went. A little part of me shriveled up and turned gray as I took my place in line.

And yet, I refuse to throw Lenny away. He sits propped up on one of the shelves in my closet. He's brown and worn from the years of upside-down and cross-eyed love. I notice him whenever I pick out anything from my closet. He tells me what to wear, to dress the part of myself. He winks three times, which means something in the language we once created.

NATIONAL FISHING DAY

Taylor's blonde hair blasts out her Jeep's sunroof. It streams into her eyes and mouth. She uses one knee to steer, freeing up her hands for air drums. She drums and screams the lines of the Offspring's "The Kids Are Not Alright". I shove my head out the passenger window like a dog high on summer.

We're on our way to her mother's house. Her mom lives in Carpentersville, in one of the many run-down houses in the woods. She's leaving for a trip with her boyfriend this weekend and has asked us to housesit.

Taylor and I live for the weekends when we can jam in that musty, water-stained basement. We jam and forget the hours. Then we'll sit on the burnt orange couch under a cloud of smoke, discussing how to improve and what to try next.

I sing and play keyboards while she bashes on the drum set her dad gave her for her sixteenth birthday. Since we've only begun to learn our instruments, none of our noise makes any sense. Luckily the houses in this neighborhood are spread so far apart that no one notices our band's horrific birthing cries.

We've written one song together. It's in honor of my ex-boyfriend, who lied about being the drummer of the band Switchfoot before they'd become famous. He had given me a blank CD with three songs on it; I'd immediately slipped into my Walkman.

I had stared into his moon-pale face and waited for Scotty's cymbals to shatter into my headphones. When the chorus line hit, I surged with awe and pride. My boyfriend was, like, a legit musician. And at just fifteen.

Scotty pouted bashfully and asked me in his smoky, baritone voice, "What do you think, babe?"

"Uh, I think you guys are good. Like real good," I said. He wore a chain-link necklace that made his entire person smell like metal. When he leaned in to kiss me, I tasted the metal on his thin, soft lips.

It was not even a month later when I heard the same song, "Meant to Live", on my mom's car radio. The band was from San Diego. Scotty had barely been outside Illinois, save for a few trips to the Dells with his family. I called him up, my voice shaking with anger.

"I just heard your song on the radio. Apparently you're in the band Switchfoot? You fucking liar," I said.

The line went silent for several seconds before Scotty said, "I think we need to break up," and hung up on me.

The driveway crackles under the Jeep's tires as we pull into Taylor's mom's gravel driveway. There's duct tape on the screen door, which her hundred-pound coonhound most likely head-butted a hole into.

"Ready to rock?" Taylor asks me.

125

"Oh, I'm ready, Freddy," I say.

The living room is the same as it was the last time we were here. Dim lights, fringed lampshades, tree ring coasters, dusty thrift store knick-knacks. Except for the shiny taxidermy catfish that sits propped up on a shelf—it looks like Shelly, Taylor's mom, added a monocle to its left eye.

"Do you want a beer?" Taylor asks.

"For sure."

Taylor reaches into a barren fridge and pulls out a can of Bud Lite. She hands it to me. I crack it open and let the cold cat piss slide down my throat.

"Nothing like a cold beer," I say, shaking my head.

"Yeah, dude."

It's funny how much Taylor and I talk to each other like we're bros. We refuse to say things girly girls might say. And yet our current phraseology sits on my lips like stray dog hair.

Taylor and I met last year in the middle of our high school foyer. It's the place where all the goth kids hang out. We don't necessarily identify with

126

their music and clothing, but this is the designated area for other weirdoes. So naturally we congregated with the rest of our fellow misfits and stood around with dead stares. We shared earbuds and scribbled into notebooks.

Eventually we started slipping out during lunch. Once we dodged the school's fat security guy, Tim, we'd drive around the neighborhood forest preserve. Taylor would always let me take the first hit off the bowl she named Dumbledore.

One day, we were tanning on a picnic bench, and a fisherman walked out of a bush.

"Afternoon, ladies," he said and scurried off to another spot along the lake. We said nothing and held our breath.

I hoped he didn't smell our weed. I had been arrested for it once before, and I wasn't about to write another thousand-word essay entitled Why I Will Not Possess Marijuana.

Another fisherman emerged from the same bush. He gave us a head nod and carried along.

Soon a whole herd of fishermen appeared. Some were small, others wore patchy beards, one guys' boots were untied. There had to be like fifteen fisherman total.

"What is it, fucking National Fishing Day?" I asked Taylor.

She snorted, and the both of us started rolling around together on the picnic bench.

"You know," she said, wiping a tear from her eye, "National Fishing Day would make a good band name."

Taylor and I head downstairs into her mom's basement. The floorboards cry out in agony with every step we take.

Once we settle onto the burnt orange couch, she opens her messenger bag and pulls out Dumbledore. She packs it tightly, using the end of her lighter to weld the top layer of green. She passes the ceramic wizard over to me.

I choke on my hit, and she pats me on the back until my lungs settle. We sit quietly together, my eyes wandering back and forth from the silver drum set behind her head to her face. She has a long, ghostly face with acne and intense eyes, which concentrate on mine. The look on her face is amused and something else.

Finally, she says, "Let's pick up where we left off?"

Our instruments are right where we left them, in the center of the room on the faded bohemian rug. I flick on the amp connected to my keyboard, and Taylor pounds out some quick warm-ups.

After an hour of what sounds like kids banging on pots and pans, we have that moment when you're in musical harmony for the first time.

She'd finally got the snare drum roll down. I had been patiently playing the same three chords and singing the same parts over and over again until her beat slipped right into mine. It was the middle of the afternoon, and the sun crept into the room in a dusty sheet. I was elated. So this is what jamming is like, I thought.

I closed my eyes and leaned into words of heartbreak and life after my first and only boyfriend. When I opened my eyes, Taylor was smiling at me. This was a proud moment for the both of us.

We find the money Shelly left us for pizza sitting on the kitchen table. Taylor invites me into her room, where we sit on her childhood bed. There are Lisa Frank posters. Hearts around all the NSYNC members. Gel pens.

Taylor's parents split up when she was in grade school, just like mine. Except hers had a quick and clean Band-Aid rip; mine preferred a long, drawn out bloodbath.

I think about Taylor sitting in this room with the newfound knowledge that her family wanted to separate. She would move in with her dad. And her sister, Tara, would stay here with her mom. I wonder if Taylor blamed herself, if she plotted ways to get everyone back together again.

"Here," she places Dumbledore in my hand again. One more hit later, neither of us can stop laughing.

"Holy shit, we were so *in sync* today, huh?" I
say eyeballing the boy band poster behind her head.

"You're such a dork," she says. "But you're my
dork."

She places her hand on mine, and we stare at it
on the paisley print bedspread. When I look up, her
face begins to inch toward mine until our noses are
touching. Her lips crackle into a smile. I pull away.

"I'm sorry," she says, looking down into her
lap.

"Don't be," I say. My hands are shaking, but I
manage to lift one and place it around the back of
her neck. My fingers grab for her knotty hair, and
her whole body surges into mine. She offers me her
tongue, which I accept into my mouth.

We fall back into her bed, the springs
screeching loudly. Everything on the walls melts
around us until we're doused in all its color. For a
second I think I hear our song coming from the
basement. Her long limbs wrap around me, and her
fingers press every note on my skin. They slip
between my legs, and we're in harmony again. And

then I lose control of my breath and my leg spasms. My face collapses into her clavicle.

A buzzer goes off in my head, like the one you hear on *Jeopardy* when someone says the wrong answer.

"What the fuck just happened?" I demand, flinging myself from her bed.

"Dude, it's okay. It's called an orgasm. Haven't you ever had one of those before?"

"Yeah, but not with a girl. This just feels weird, okay? You know what, I think we need to get a guy in this band. Okay?"

"Okay, okay, Sarah." She looks down into her lap again. Her ears are two cherries on the side of her head.

"There's this guy in my math class who plays guitar. I could ask him."

"Splendid. I'm going to sleep on the couch, alright?"

"Yeah, whatever you want."

I feel like a bitch, but that wasn't supposed to happen. Although I've had the same euphoria tons of times by myself, no boy has ever made me do what Taylor just did with grace and ease.

I had a best friend named Hannah when I was six years old. *The Little Rascals* had just come out. We reenacted the whole scene where Alfalfa sneaks Darla into the He Man Woman Haters club. Hannah played Darla, and I was Alfalfa. Hannah's mom walked in on us puckering up for a kiss.

"Absolutely not!" she screamed, wrenching me off Hannah like I was a snake coiling up around her. "You two are friends. Friends don't kiss!"

I wasn't allowed to see Hannah for a whole month. Finally, Hannah's mom lifted the ban and invited me over for another play date with her daughter. I had to apologize and tell everyone that what we did was wrong.

It's the middle of the night, and I'm thirsty. I stumble into the kitchen, opening up several cabinets in search of a glass before I find the right one.

I jump at the sound of the back door opening. Taylor appears in the doorway. Her hood is up, and she glances up at me. Her face looks swollen. She attempts to move past me, but I block her.

"Hey."

"Hey," she whimpers like a puppy. I feel like the world's biggest asshole.

"Heyyyy," I say, embracing her thin rail of a body. "Hey, it's okay."

"I just... I just don't want to lose your friendship."

"That's not gonna happen, I swear," I say.

The next time we take the Jeep up to Taylor's mom's house, Bobby is with us. He's the guitarist Taylor was talking about. He's short, with glasses and a turtle like posture. He can play Van Halen's "Eruption" with his eyes closed.

What can I say? National Fishing Day needed a guitar player. Sometimes when all three of us are playing in sync, the whole room vibrates and it feels like we're the very center of energy. I'll look up and catch Taylor's eye, her cantaloupe-slice smile.

"Dude!" she shouts when the song's all over.

"Dude," Bobby and I'll agree.

MEET ME IN THE STACKS

I've "worked" at the Cypress Grove Public Library for the last nine years. I'm not a very good employee.

Don't get me wrong—I'll shelve a cart of books or two and tidy up my assigned sections, but in between duties I float from conversation to conversation.

I have a system. First, I'll hit up Debbie in the Adult section. She's the person in charge of checking out computers in the technology lab. In between her assisting elderly patrons in opening a new tab on their browser or unjamming the printer for a flustered student, we'll discuss her obese cat, Barry. Barry has diabetes. She once showed me how to administer a shot to the back of his neck.

Debbie still doesn't know about the party at her house last summer. Or that I'm a terrible influence on her son, who thankfully hasn't picked up any of my habits like smoking, swearing, and chewing my nails down to stubs and spitting them onto the carpet. He's a sensitive boy who likes pop music, water parks, and browsing the aquatic animal books in my section. Eels (Section 597.43) are his favorite.

Then I'll head over to the book drop and sort the books that people returned from the night before. My favorite day to sort books is on Sundays with Sam. She has a lip ring and a diehard love for a few emo bands she'll take off work for and drive across the country to support. I once drew her a portrait of Davey Havok of AFI, getting the dramatic swoop of his bangs just right.

Sam and I had a fling one summer that ended with her going to the movies on a date with my cousin to get back at me. I felt like a real asshole. I just couldn't decide whether or not I wanted to be in a relationship with my blue-eyed, gaslighting first love, Tom Shindel. Sam and I still talk though—just not about what it feels like to take turns lying in each other's lap. We talk about the weather, books—we don't understand why there are so many James Patterson novels in existence. It's ridiculous really.

It's hard not to make friends among these hallowed stacks. There's Marcy, who started a vintage clothing company a few months ago. Everything she wears is from another time—a simpler one, as they say. Stitched vests, baggy sweaters, pointed shoes—the girl could rock anything, honestly. Jenna's a big mushball who makes everyone homemade cards for every holiday and hosts bonfires in her backyard every summer. She desperately wants to be liked, and we reassure her that we more than like her.

There's the lanky, cool Bart, who often brings a set of drumsticks and practices for his band, Ratbag. We all crush on him pretty hard. Even some of the older women blush when he breezes by the desk with a courteous "hello" and "how are you." He's a punk rocker with manners. Is there a better combination? I don't think so.

My voice tends to carry, which upsets some of the librarians who feel no shame in laying down the law like Judge Judies.

We attempt to stifle our laughter, comment on all the townies, and read to each other from the books we're supposed to be shelving. There's no shortage of topics to chew the fat about. We chew on everything from ways to orgasm to Harry Potter fanfiction to the general fucked-upness of the world.

We know all the regulars, like the Anime twins, who we suspect may be the ones responsible for ripping pages of nude characters from graphic novels that require parental consent to check out. Then there's the infamous FeeFee, one of the misbehaved little heathens who likes to ride barefoot on his Razor scooter through the nonfiction section.

We're all responsible for keeping the play area clean. It's become this silent competition to see who cleans up best by the end of the day. Bruce, a mostly mute, large-boned coworker, somehow manages to stuff himself into the small children's playhouse and empty out all its cubbies of books. "No one does toys like Bruce," the librarians like to tell the rest of us rubes.

If you need to know anything about the Dewey Decimal System, I'm your girl. The section I'm responsible for houses the 500s, which has books on dinosaurs—everyone's favorite. This section—567.9 specifically—is a slop fest. I can never seem to get it organized the way I want it. Especially that stupid Stegosaurus-shaped book.

Many of the women who work here like to Mom me. They ask me a lot of questions about my colorful home life, which for most part I've managed to keep private from them.

I stay away from the gossipy hens (Section 636.5) in circulation just as well as I stay away from the malicious gab circles in school. Really, what else do these women have to do besides check in books and cluck about the latest happenings between poor Anna, another co-worker, and her alcoholic husband? I like Pearl, though. She's quiet and has kind, Disney-shaped eyes. She once found me sobbing and eating Taco Bell in my car before a shift and asked me if I needed a hug. It was a good hug.

I'm surprised I'm still allowed to work here. I call up my friends and ask them to come visit me. I do conspicuous things under my cart, like write poems (Poetry: Sections 811 & 818) and wolf down burritos (Mexican food: Section 641.5972). Parents have complained to the front desk about my audible profanities. I even lied about knowing my boyfriend when he applied for a job, which is against work policy. My boss caught us making out in an aisle and made sure we never worked another shift together ever again.

During my last annual review, she let me know she knew when I was lying on my timesheet. She said, "Sarah, I should probably fire you, but I want to give you another chance."

I assume it's over for me for good when I use the library printer to pump out fifty copies of my grandfather's eulogy. We're supposed to pay for ink, just like the patrons. It's ten cents per page, so technically, I'm stealing. Wouldn't be the first or last time.

Somewhere there's a Kohl's that I'm banned from entering for life.

My grandfather's suffering had been short-lived, thankfully, but the sadness was starting to set in like a fog over my life.

It's Eugene, the sweaty IT guy, who catches me hunched over the printer in the dark back office. He adjusts his thick-rimmed glasses and wags his finger. Eugene has always been a stickler for the rules.

"You know you're not supposed to be in here, right?" He has the kind of voice that sounds like there's always something lodged in the back of his throat.

I don't know what it is exactly about this moment of being caught after hundreds of transgressions that especially stings, but it does. I can see my boss's long, disapproving face and hear our last chance conversation echo through my head. It's only a matter of time before this encounter makes it down the grapevine.

"My grandpa's dead, Eugene," I say and shove a warm copy into his arms. There's a small picture on the front of it. My grandpa's wearing his blue sweater with olive stains on it; his false teeth glisten. I collect the rest of my pile from the printer and scurry past him without giving him time to retort.

"It was nice knowing you girls," I tell a bewildered Marcy and Jenna, who are folding Starburst wrappers together at a table in the break room.

This is the sacred place where we ate shitty TV dinners and where *Wheel of Fortune* or tired baseball games a few people cared about was always playing. Once a year we line every table and countertop in this room with stuff we find lying around our houses and bid on each other's junk. It's

142

a jolly time for all the hoarders and sentimentalists among us.

"Sarah, what's the matter?" they ask, but it's too late. I'm already manhandling my belongings out of a locker.

I've spent a third of part of my life in this library. It gave me so much. And I just took and took. I shove myself outside the heavy employee door that scrapes the sidewalk whenever anyone opens it. The wind is cold on my face, which is hot with shame.

Later, I learn that almost all of my coworkers read the eulogy I cobbled together for my family in honor of the man so many of us loved. He used to visit me here at the library, ask for recommendations on books to read, and generally charm the pants off everyone he came into contact with. He'd ask about their families and days like he meant it. They thought he was just adorable.

My grandpa was one part of my home life that I didn't feel the need to hide or control—probably

143

because he never exercised that need on me. And now he's gone, and I feel like I'm fading in places.

Marcy, Jenna, my boss, a few circulation ladies, and others show up at his wake. I was nearly shaking reading the words I wrote about him. They rattled and bounced around the funeral home, richotted off all the crucifixes. Tears filled the room where he rested peacefully.

When elephants (Section 599.674) come across the remains of another elephant, even if that elephant did not belong to their herd, they touch the bones with their trunks and cover them up with leaves and grass. As my friends surrounded me and my grieving loved ones, I realized that my herd was bigger than I'd known.

INTERSECTION

The police receive a call on a woman in the middle of an intersection directing traffic to collide. Under the red lights, she begs for fire. She curses the world around her and points her fingers at the commuters opening and closing their mouths like fish cast onto land.

A youngish officer with wispy hair exits his car. He moves his lips, silently moving and reciting rehearsed protocol. He calls to her. When she doesn't hear him, he reaches and latches onto her shoulders. He asks the meaning of her actions. She coughs so hard she has to spit into the road. She says she doesn't know why she's here. She scans the street signs for answers. Drivers creep by.

When I open the front door, my mother slinks past me with one shoulder brushing the wall and eyes to the floor. She wears skinny like she doesn't want to take up too much room. I thank the officers. The bald one who has been here many times asks if I'm eighteen yet. I laugh like I mean it.

I set a glass of milk on her nightstand. She lies in bed with her feet propped on her pillow. I slip into bed next to her. I twirl her loosened hair with my fingers. Tears roll down her cheeks. She smiles. I smile back. It's like looking in a drooping mirror, if Dalí made mirrors instead of clocks. I fight the urge to look away.

WHOOPIE PIE

I usually assemble my lunch first thing every morning—half a sandwich, yogurt, banana, and some nuts. Sometimes, when I'm feeling like a badass, I pack a piece of chocolate.

Then there are other days when I am so mind-numbingly lazy I don't want to pack anything. On those days getting out of bed is first priority.

We've all been there. We throw off the blankets and stretch longer than we have to. We play tug-of-war with ourselves. We stand in front of our closets with blank stares. We haven't had our coffee yet, and already it hurts to think about the rest of the day.

On days like that I'm forced to go out for lunch and spend more money, even though I have perfectly good groceries in the fridge. My usual spot for those lazy days is Corner Bakery. It's cozy and doesn't have to explain itself to my wallet. I like the lentil soup because it doesn't skimp on the mushrooms, and the warm spiciness soothes my entire body. I like to feel the heat in my ears. I stand at the fountain drink dispensary, tilt my cup sideways like I learned in my server days, and fill my cup with Diet Coke until it kisses the top.

A server bustles past me. She has a stack of dirty dishes piled high—a napkin from her pile floats like a feather to the floor. She disappears into the back. I stare at the napkin on the floor. I reach down, pick it up, and throw it away. My rationalization is that I saw it fall, I'm standing right next to it, and the garbage can is four steps away from me.

As I'm shoving a lemon into my drink, a woman with red hair in a messy bun taps me on the shoulder. I recognize her; she has served me before.

"Excuse me, but I've been here for five years, and I can't remember the last time a customer picked anything up off the floor." She looks bewildered. She peers at me like I just performed CPR on a battered puppy I rescued from a burning building. I'm slightly confused by her demeanor.

In grade school my teachers gave us prizes if we were "caught doing something good". One teacher gave away pieces of toffee he called "tastations", which made them sound even more delicious than they already were. To my surprise, I received a "tastation" after volunteering to deliver homework to a fellow classmate who was sick at home with mono. In my eleven-year-old brain I assumed it would be a weekly homework for candy exchange. Turned out, it was a one-time offer. Point was, I was noticed, and it felt good to be noticed, especially when it wasn't my main objective. Or maybe it was just the candy.

Then, you grow up. Sometimes you do nice things, and good things happen. Sometimes not.

Ultimately, there's no reward as satisfying as a tasty "tastation".

The redheaded server looks at me. I swear I can almost see the thin layer of ice in her eyes melting as she cracks a smile at me and offers a strand of words I will never forget: "Here's a free whoopie pie." I stare at her one wayward tooth as she enunciates each syllable.

I briefly wonder if she's making an example out of me so that the other customers feel like shit. But "Huh?" is all I can muster.

"Here, take it. Thank you. Seriously, thank you."

I fumble with the flaky pastry. In the center of the tart sandwich, there's a white heart palpitating, a pasty pile of cream thicker than a deck of cards. Not to mention, it's adorable. Whoever made this pie had kissed it on its forehead and neatly tucked it away in a thin wrapper. This thing was made to be held, then ravaged, like a burrito.

I feel like a hero. Several people smile at me on my way out the revolving door. I puff out my chest

150

like a robin in springtime. I feel a little like Clark
Kent ready to take on a day filled with villains and
disasters, and people to save.

I sit at a table outside and relish my lunch with
more vigor than usual, saving my prize for last. The
sun is shining—and oh my, what a lovely little
breeze!

Suddenly a bee lands on the lid of my cup. It
crawls with thread-like limbs up my straw. I shoo it
away as another bee—probably its wingman–lands
on the paper wrapped around my whoopie pie.

No big deal. I collect my things and move to
another table. They smell me. They remember my
name. They follow.

People tell you to never swat a bee, but I felt
made of steel, so I rolled up the papers I brought for
reading material and slammed the scroll down onto
the table. Over and over again, I defended what I
had rightfully earned. After all, I had picked up a
napkin. Not anyone else. Me. I had saved the day!
It's my fucking whoopie pie!

I notice my forehead is swimming in sweat— and that there's a family silently waiting behind me, frozen with terror on the sidewalk. I hold my fire. I slump my arm down to my side. I move for them to pass me. They shuffle along and avoid eye contact.

I return inside, where there's no endless breeze or intoxicating sunshine. "The bees tried to eat my pie. I tried to kill them," I told another server.

"Yeah, I know what you mean. It seems they've developed a sort of... resilience. I can't clean the tables anymore. Even the mess belongs to them. You made the right choice."

I sink my teeth into the whoopie pie and imagine a list of desserts, the rewards of my youth. I cackle at the spectacle of poor old Sarah swatting away. And then I stop thinking. I let each bite settle in my teeth and give them a buzz.

FIRE & LICE

"Just cut it off," Lee says.

"Are you sure?"

"Yeah."

Lee's damp hair hangs over the tub, which is peppered with the dead bugs I've just scraped from her scalp with a metal-toothed comb.

"Party's over, boys," I say, taunting the unwanted visitors who have overstayed their welcome on her head.

Hours earlier, Lee called me on the phone, asking me to pick her up from her friend's house. As I pulled into the half-finished driveway, she stood in the garage wearing a plastic bag on her head. Two plump tears rolled down her cheek.

I cut Lee's hair with the same pair of scissors I've used to shred chicken. It's the only pair I own. Her hair fans open and piles into a heap in the tub.

Lee has let me cut her hair once before, when we were kids. I'd discovered a pair of scissors my mom lost in the underground cavern of the sink.

"We're going to be twins," I told Lee. I hacked away at our hair until we looked like mutants. I thought we were a masterpiece, but the horror etched into my mother's face said otherwise. The next day at school was picture day.

"Lice. I'm so disgusting," Lee whimpers.

"It's okay, Lee. It could happen to anyone."

Lee has been jumping couches during her winter break, and this week she's staying by me. She's not allowed over by my father's house after giving my stepmother the middle finger in the middle of dinner. And she and my mother haven't spoken in years.

The chemical foam I spray into my hands crackles and expands. I smear it all over Lee's head, running my fingers from her roots all the way down to the edges of her chestnut brown hair.

"I'm sorry," she says.

"Stop saying sorry."

After I wash my entire wardrobe and vacuum every crevice of my house, I collapse onto my bed. In my dreams, my head itches. I scratch it and begin to pull out chunks of what feels like tree bark. I hold each piece in my hand and examine it. I realize they are honeycombs. Inside each comb is a black bee. All of them are dead.

When I awake, it's still dark, and my head feels like it's on fire. I slip into the bathroom and stare into the mirror. My eyes look like two pufferfish. I have to get ready for work in an hour.

I have this prickling feeling that I have lice, or that I will have them soon. Even though I did everything I was supposed to do. I searched the internet for support, following the instructions left by every mom whose kid came home from school one day with a head full of microscopic assholes.

I learned a lot about lice. Like how a female can lay up to six eggs on a head and drink blood from it five times per day. That their eggs stick like glue to a person's hair. Or that they can hold their breath underwater.

I also watched the worst case of lice ever caught on video. Seeing them all clumped together is enough to make anyone dry heave a little.

I throw away my favorite furry rug that used to greet my feet every morning. Nothing is clean enough. I tilt my head and listen to my hair for tiny movements.

Then finally, I see one. A piece of brown rice waltzing around my hairbrush.

I lather my head twice a day, and Lee and I pick at each other's heads like two baboons. This is the most amount of time we've spent together in years.

It had been a wrecking ball of a week. We were going through the over-the-counter stuff like fiends. In the Walgreens parking lot, I back my car into another car. The driver steps out of her vehicle and shakes two open palms at me.

"Didn't you see me? Didn't you hear me honking?" she demands.

"Lady, I have lice!" I scream. My right eye begins to twitch. I realize I'm wearing my pink house slippers. She backs away slowly, gets into her car and drives away.

Finally, Lee and I get our hands on some medical-grade shit, which wipes out the entire population.

Even with the lice gone, we're on edge with each other. It's like I'm living with a teenager. Lee is bored. Lee wants to borrow my car. Lee needs a cigarette or a drink. Lee needs a lot of drinks, actually. When did she start drinking this much?

On Christmas, I catch her in my boyfriend's parent's kitchen, pouring shot after shot of whiskey into a little glass and tossing it back like it's water. Her eyes are piercingly blue and wayward.

"That's enough, Lee," I say quiet enough so no one in the other room hears.

When I reach out to grab the glass from her, she dumps the liquid into my face. My eyes sting as I watch her walk out the door.

She disappears for two days; I find her on my front steps. I don't recognize her for a second. Her entire head is shaved.

157

"I knew the lice were gone, but I just couldn't shake the feeling. So I pulled a Britney," she laughs. "Is it bad?"

"Not really, actually. You pull it off," I say.

I offer her a cigarette, which we pass back and forth.

"I'm sorry I've been annoying. Derek broke up with me a few weeks ago. It was so easy for him to throw me away, you know?" she says.

"What an idiot," I tell her, placing a hand on her knee. She flinches at my touch.

I was so distracted by her head that this is the first time I notice two red engravings on her arm. And her overgrown toenails. And that she's wearing gray flip-flops, an enlarged hoodie and a pair of tattered basketball shorts.

Lee is the most sensitive person I know. She cries openly at songs or movies and talks to people in the checkout line like I do—but in a TMI kind of way. Sometimes, it embarrasses me. Sometimes, I have to remind myself that she feels things more deeply than a lot of others.

158

She's also braver than me. She's only twenty-four, and she's already held the hands of two people on their deathbeds. One was a woman with Alzheimer's. Another was my grandfather. She stayed in his hospice room until he breathed his last sweet breath.

I hope that, if it ever comes down to it, I'm brave enough to stay in the room for her.

"Hey, do you wanna get a few things from the store before you go back to school?" I ask.

My sister floats around Target's dressing room in her new clothes. She's modeling a shirt that hugs her middle and flows from the bottom, accentuating her hips. She runs her fingers along the sewn parts of the fabric, smiling in the mirror at her reflection.

In the checkout line, Lee tells an elderly woman all about her new haircut.

"My friend used her dog's clippers to shave it," she tells her. "I think it's pretty rad. Kind of freeing, you know?"

The woman smiles politely and begins to place her items onto the belt.

The day I drop Lee off at the train station is bittersweet. I don't know who she will meet or what she will do at school this semester, and if she will lie to me about any of it. I try to telepathically communicate with her, like we tried to do so many times when we were kids. Maybe she will listen to my sisterly advice if I don't say anything at all.

Lee and I stare at each other for several minutes in my car. She has a face that children gape at and want to touch. She has freckles on her nose, big, oceanic eyes, and a gap in her teeth.

I can't tell if the tears are filling her eyes or my own.

RESOLUTIONS

A woman wedges herself between the section of the register where customers shouldn't go. She's clearly ignoring the unwritten rules of grocery store lines. We know these people. They're everywhere. Sometimes we're them.

After she pays and turns to leave, she realizes something was wrong. She pivots, cuts off the cashier midsentence—just as she's in the middle of asking me if Old-Fashioned Donut is a good flavor of coffee. I don't get the chance to tell her that, yes, it's delicious.

The customer—a pasty, middle-aged woman with offensive blonde highlights—insists to the cashier—a stout Indian woman with braces—that her receipt is flawed. The cashier asks the woman to wait a moment while she finishes ringing me up. The woman acquiesces with a dramatic huff.

It's the customer who addresses me as the cashier scans my ID for the wine on the belt in front of me.

"How old are you?" she asks, her eyes narrowing. She might as well not have gotten out of bed today.

I tell her I'm twenty-four because I've already forgotten that I turned twenty-five two days ago.

"Are you sure you're twenty-four? You look twenty to me."

I want to ask her who the fuck cares, but I say *Uhhh, thank you* instead.

"You look young. You're good. You're okay."

Some older people think that all young people are okay. They need them to be okay. They need to believe that there was once a time when they themselves were okay. This is the mutiny of adulthood. Adults don't realize that blind reassurance robs young people of real doubts, fears,

162

and insecurities that they need to admit are there before the next stage of their transition.

I want to tell this woman that I've been smoking cigarettes since I was in the womb. I want to tell her I'm in love with grown men who encourage me to be my best self, and I have mothered people far older than me. I want to say that sometimes I get so close to the core of people that I can't breathe. I catch colds, cough my brains out. It wears my body down.

The woman's comment stays with me long after the grocery store. It follows me as I bypass Ben in the living room, ignoring his hello.

"What's wrong?" he asks and lifts one flap of his headphones. I can always tell when he's in the middle of a heated first-person shooter showdown by the way he mashes the buttons.

"I don't want to talk about it," I say, heading upstairs to my office.

I pull out the swivel chair in front of my desk and slap open a pad of paper, willing myself to pen some resolutions. Even though I am at a point where I'm forgetting my age, I can't fight the New Year mentality no matter how hard I try. My body has been following through on resolutions I did not openly make. I didn't even smoke a cigarette today.

I told my best friend I wanted to take a vow of silence. Maybe that should be my first resolution.

"What would you do with yourself, if you had to just stand at the cash register and nod politely at the cashier?" she asked.

It's true. She knows me. I don't mix well with silence. But sometimes I wish I said more on paper than I do in person.

If I just cut some more of the excess, I could get to know the person of my own invention. *This is it,* I think. I straighten up in my chair and begin to press black ink onto the page.

Write your book

This has been haunting my resolution list for years.

Are you too scattered to write a book? Do people even read anymore? What could you possibly say that hasn't already been said? The familiar doubts and excuses that plague writers eat away at me, too.

I once had a marketing manager who told me to write everything down in fifty words or less. I panicked. I gave him more than he'd asked for. He looked bored when I handed him my article and popped a wad of gum in his mouth, chewing anxiously.

He wasn't wrong in some ways, you know? Everything needs to be clickable, follow-worthy these days.

But I can't shake the thought: what if I write, if just for me? What if what I say could connect with just one other person?

Clean one thing a day

I have another friend, who just so happens to have been raised by a very strict Polish mother, who helped me clean my kitchen about a month ago. Bless her soul. She swore that what I insisted was dirt was actually mold, and then fairy-dusted Comet Bleach Powder all over the place. She hopped on top of my counters like a private investigator, frowning into cabinets, reaching for expired food, and rearranging items by size and color.

"Why do you have three different bottles of oregano?"

"Easy. I thought I ran out."

The main reason I have yet to clean my kitchen is that I'm lazy. But my go-to reason is the way this kitchen was built, which is very inconvenient. For one, I need a stool to reach every shelf above the first one. That, and some drawers don't even open. Some give the illusion that they're bigger and more functional than they actually are.

Everything in my home exists in a designated pile, and I'm okay but not okay with that. "Housework, when done right, will kill you," Erma Bombeck said. It's stuck with me over the years.

Volunteer for something you're passionate about

Last year, I volunteered to tutor inner-city kids. Once a week I'd help one kid, Carlos, muddle through *Hop on Pop*. Every week he'd read just a little bit faster. I could tell his teacher took her time on him.

Carlos told me that Spanish makes him feel stupid, and he'd been trying to forget it. I told him to never forget his language, that the adults all have it wrong. We should be learning his too.

He's the kind of kid who is big for his age. He has a haircut like Sonic the Hedgehog. It just grows that way. His ferrety friend Frankie put it best: "You look like one of those big, dumb bullies that are in movies. But you're actually not a bully or dumb, you're really nice, and you're my friend."

Kids are masters of disjointed compliments.

Another thing Carlos said that stuck with me: he said he wished he were rich, so he could buy all the Legos in the world. I can't remember if I liked listening to him read or watch him play with Legos more.

Get a therapist

Therapy is a laughable concept in my circle of family and friends. But many of them don't seem to want to do the same digging that I feel compelled to do.

My childhood burns my fingers whenever I touch it. I find my mother running away to California beaches. I find my father getting drunk in the storage locker where all his things are. I listen to the words in my brother's scream. I find a way back to the bunk bed I slept on, with my sister underneath me, for years. I remember I was afraid the top bunk would crush her, but I never offered to switch beds. I worry that twenty-five is too old to be coming to grips with my past. But I have a feeling reconciliation is the only way to go.

I'm learning that the older I get, the more I see the distinction between feeling crazy and being crazy. But then, the harder I think about the concept, the more the two blur into one. I have a fear that I will go crazy.

We all are crazy to some degree, and especially at certain points of our lives, but most people isolate themselves in their own crazy, enhancing it.

Sometimes I sit at my desk at work and feel like I'm going to collapse, like I'm going to forget my name.

I worry about crossing over and getting stuck in the most convoluted version of myself.

Will I float away?

Ben knocks on the door. Sometimes I forget there's anyone on the other side of it. This room is the Virginia Woolf style fortress of discovery I've built for myself. There's a map of the world on one wall, a flimsy three-dollar Target sign that urges me to "create" on another. My favorite tree grows older outside my window.

Ben stands in my white-framed doorway. He seems so far away.

"How do you feel about getting some margaritas from Maria's?" he asks me. "I want to hear about your day."

He has soft, sea-green eyes that want to know things. I want to tell him about my day this time. I want to share my resolutions over chips and salsa with him, tell him why this batch is more meaningful than the last.

BLACK DOG

I poke my head out the window like it's a toe about to be dipped into water. The air is warm, so the chill of hesitation must be my own. How unusual for February. Everyone knows there's something screwy going on with these snowless Midwest winters.

I suggest a place near my house where my brother, nephew, and I can walk. The nature center, with its sunflower garden, charming barn, and prairie grasses, is the only thing that feels like country in this buzzing suburb large enough to be a city.

Every now and then I escape its daily programming. Men who drive sports cars with tinted windows think they own these streets. I can't see their eyes as they drive by. I can only hear their music, feel the barrels of bass they send rolling down the street.

Cameron zips up his hoodie and sifts through his pockets for a lighter.

"Hey, can I bum a cigarette?" he asks me. "I only have half of one left."

"I quit," I tell him as I shove my feet into a pair of gym shoes.

"Oh, again?"

"I'm trying," I say, which is only half true. I've quit for the third time this month.

Dylan presses his head into his dad's leg. He rubs his eye, and I wonder if this means he didn't have a nap. His hair runs wild. A glob of it sits in one place, revealing a rosy first scar on his forehead—the result of a hot cup of coffee he pulled from a high countertop. The boy who lived. There's dirt caked underneath each of his long fingernails.

"Are you ready?" Cameron asks. He clears the phlegm from the back of his throat and holds it in his mouth before swallowing.

I slip the strap of the diaper bag onto my shoulder, and Cameron plops Dylan into a stroller with one crooked wheel.

Outside, my neighbor walks her dachshund, its nose glued to the grass. The poor thing looks like a stuffed eggplant, wearing a knitted purple dog sweater. I have yet to talk to this neighbor, or any neighbor, though I've been here close to a year.

Last week, I glared at her for tossing garbage bags onto the curb, instead of into the garbage can where they belong. Every Wednesday night, raccoons gallop through the darkness, their yellow eyes shining as they dig into the bags, pilfer for leftovers, and fling stale bagels and banana peels onto people's lawns. Beef jerky wrappers stick to bushes; shrunken apples lounge in gutters. There's something about the sight of a moldy loaf of bread resting in the middle of a driveway, and the public worker who bends over to pick it up, that infuriates me.

Sometimes I miss the camaraderie of apartment living. I used to be more conscious of the people who lived around me. I'd offer my neighbors a piece of homemade birthday cake, swap kale for blueberries, listen to an elderly woman discuss the shade of white she'd like to paint her living room, or keep my eye on a cat or two over the weekend. I didn't even mind exchanging pleasantries with the person next door who knew what I sounded like when I smashed body parts with my boyfriend.

Cameron trudges down the sidewalk, kicking rocks and clumps of dirt as I push the stroller. Dylan leans forward, then swivels his head, to check that his father isn't too far behind him. He raises his head and closes his eyelids, surrendering them to the sun.

I rifle through the diaper bag and shove a juice box into his cup holder, which he accepts with a garble. As he scoops it up, I'm reminded of a picture of my brother at two years old: kneeling on our old orange carpet, holding a juice cup with teeth marks and presenting it to the world. At twenty-three, he still has the same face.

"I've started working with a new sound mixer for my band," Cameron says.

"What happened to the old one?"

"He wasn't cutting it. The transitions were terrible."

"Ah."

"Yeah, nothing personal. He just didn't fit," he explained. "But anyway, I should have an EP by the end of this month."

Cameron is the lead screamer of a band called Ground Zeroes. The first time I listened to his music it sounded like the inside of someone's stomach, but I've come to appreciate the release and control of it. His screaming is a second language. Or first. Technically, he came into this world screaming. We all did.

There's something reassuring about my brother conjuring up caged rage and putting it in its rightful place. The aftermath doesn't include holes in drywall. Police visits. Court fees. Eviction notices. Things Cameron has put our family through that I've had to learn how to forgive.

He's always shoving earbuds into my ears, talking lightning fast about some new song that's keeping him up all night. Music has become one of the only ways that we understand each other. Yet more recently I find myself clearing my throat and changing the subject.

"Hey, did you hear back about that stocking job?" I ask.

"Still waiting to hear back."

"How about…"

"Jesus, will you let up?"

My brother is having a hard time finding a job with a felony. When he was sixteen, he stole and sold a few of my aunt's heirlooms, valuables with real family history, and used the money to buy weed. Wanting to teach him a lesson, she reported him. No one realized how long that lesson would follow him.

We reach the nature center's trailhead. On the left side of the trail, there's a dusty, single-story building alongside a fenced-in garden where sunflowers slumber. A splintered pike protrudes

175

from the middle of the garden. It reads "Green Thumb Kids' Garden". Shorter pikes surround it. There are ladybugs, dragonflies, and clovers painted onto them.

Dylan's eyes bulge. I stop grilling Cameron and focus my attention on Dylan's first nature walk. We pass the garden, and our feet hit a long boardwalk. The wayward wheel bounces around.

Plants sing silent songs of impending resurrection in the wind. Long prairie grass the color of cornhusks hangs from the sides of the boardwalk and brushes Dylan's knee. He screams in delight, his eyes two round raindrops about to burst. I swerve the stroller so that a piece of grass touches him again, and he oozes with laughter.

A rooster crow's call punctures the air. Dylan tilts his ear to listen. I've never heard a cock-a-doodle-doo in broad daylight before. He scrunches his nose at the sound, like it's not what he expected. He wriggles out of his stroller, eager to investigate.

"You ready to stretch your feet, bud?" Cameron asks him. "Hey, stay over here by us, though."

Dylan lumbers onto the trail, his stiff shoes clapping the ground. He's getting to be a professional walker, but he still lets his arms dangle behind his back, like a duck preparing for takeoff.

I think about the first time I ever held Dylan. He was wrapped tight in a blanket, a creature stirring in its cocoon. His head nestled where my bicep and forearm met.

Earlier that same summer I'd cradled a stingray in my arms. Its slippery, cool, gelatinous underside pressed against my palms. Its fins flopped over the water and its body lay flat in my hands, which were quivering just below the water. Though the terror of being stung seized me, I couldn't help but be invigorated by the life I held in my hands. It was pure intimacy to be so close to something so strange and beautiful that emerges from the sea.

After leaving the hospital, I retraced Dylan's nose, eyes, and cheeks in my head. I thought about how he'd open and close his mouth and squint like a blind baby bird. I thought about how, every now and then, he'd open his eyes and look around, waywardly, like he was drunk. That day was the first day he'd ever used his eyes.

Dylan bolts. It takes me by surprise, and I fumble with the diaper bag still dangling from my shoulder. It topples into the grass. The contents spill out, and I quickly shove them back in. I jog to catch up to Cameron, who jogs to catch up with Dylan.

Dylan sits on every bench we pass. Each of them is engraved with names and sayings like "In memory of Peggy Manning, for her love of nature and children". After he hoists himself up, Dylan presses his ear against the wood as if to listen to it. He looks at Cameron and me, and holds out his hand like he's serving a platter of food.

"What?" he asks.

"What?" we ask back.

Dylan lets us know he's had enough by throwing himself to the ground and shaking his head when we ask him to stand up.

"Welp, looks like it's time for a diaper change," Cameron announces.

"I got it," I say and pull a towel from the diaper bag.

As I place Dylan down onto the towel, he begins to flail and scream. He balls his fists and hits me in the arm, as I wrestle with his diaper. My fingers reach for the diaper cream, which I fail to locate in the bag. Dylan's cries shred the silence. Sweat dots my forehead.

Cameron scratches his head impatiently. "Will you just give him to me?" he says.

"I'm fine. I just can't find the diaper cream. I think I may have lost it when I dropped the bag."

Dylan's howls bounce off trees and rocks.

"You're not his fucking mom, you know, so like… you can stop," Cameron says.

I turn to look at Cameron. His eyes used to be bluer, lighter, less cold. I shove the diaper into his hands and tell him, "I'll be right back. I'm going to go grab the cream. I know where I dropped it."

I don't want Cameron to actually know what's on the tip of my tongue—that I actually don't want a relationship with him at all, that the only reason I'm still in his life is Dylan.

It terrifies me to think what my nephew would think of me if he knew I had been one of the people who had advocated against him coming into the world. My brother, after all, had been living out of my car shortly before Dylan was conceived. It had been a hard time, a dark time, when he was born.

Dylan, please, please forgive me for this: when I found out about you, I was sad. I was not on board. I was afraid you wouldn't be able to get what you deserve.

When I get back to the spot I left Cameron and Dylan, they're gone.

I backtrack. Then I head down the part of the trail we had yet to explore together. No sign of them anywhere. I call their names, elongate the syllables.

A breeze twirls my hair, reminding me to relax, but I can't. Where could they possibly have gone?

I walk. I pass the garden, the cars in the parking lot. I start toward home, checking the city's nooks along the way. Maybe Dylan is sitting on the benches by the outdoor art exhibit.

Something soft mushrooms underneath my shoe.

"Oh good. I just stepped in shit," I announce to no one.

I can't even muster a laugh. I scrape my shoe into the grass. A car passes me and honks. I flip them the bird with one hand and continue to scrape with the other.

When my brother was younger, he used to have a recurring nightmare about the tortured *Lord of the Rings* creature, Gollum, slipping in through his window. He'd shake me awake and beg me to let him sleep in my room with me and Lee. She disapproved, of course, but I'd always sneak him in, and he'd curl up on the floor near where I slept in the bottom bunk. I felt relieved by his presence. When all three of us slept in the same room, I knew who I was.

I wrench the diaper bag back onto my shoulder, shove my foot into my shoe, and continue to walk.

By the time I hit the last two blocks before my street, the sky turns black and blue. Clouds layer on top of each other, reminding me of a diorama. I hear leaves crinkle.

I turn around to see a black, furry mass in the grass behind me. It's a dog. He's not wearing a collar. Yet he has a broad belly and glossy coat. I lower myself to the ground, put my head down, and put my hand out so he can smell me. He bobs toward me, sniffs my fingers, and bows his head for me to pet him.

"Hey bud, where are your humans? Huh?" I scratch behind his ears.

There's something off about this dog. He doesn't wag his tail. He doesn't seem happy or afraid. I've never met such an emotionless dog. I pull out a granola bar I'd been saving in my pocket. I break off a piece and shake it in front of his face. He sniffs it and lies down, uninterested.

I start to walk again, waving the granola bar at him and beckoning him to join me, but he doesn't.

It's getting darker, and he begins to blend into the grass.

"Fine, don't come," I tell him.

By the time I reach the cul-de-sac, I'm exhausted. All the lights in my home are off. No Cameron and Dylan. I step onto the curb and notice my neighbor's garbage bags sitting there. Any moment the coons will be here to claim their treasure.

Every home in this circle looks the same—same beige panels, same white lettering, same patchy, brown rooftops. Sometimes the sameness makes me want to scream. I could really use a cigarette.

The black dog plops down next to me. I scoot closer to his body. He doesn't seem to mind, so I place a hand on his back. His fur is coarser than it looks. I bury my face into it and weep.

ON CLIMBING MOUNTAINS

The sleepy shop owner, who's just sold us a flyswatter, looks at us with eyes like damp leaves when we tell him we've never hiked the Smoky Mountains before.

I run my fingers over a cedar coaster sitting on a shelf. Ben whooshes the new swatter through the air, whacking dead an imaginary fly.

"I like your work," I tell the shopkeeper.

"It keeps me off the streets," he says with a scruffy laugh.

I can tell that he's comfortable with silence as he assesses our city nerves. Ben and I ping pong our gaze around the shop, surveying all the items he made from the trees. There's an intricate wooden carving of an eagle in flight among piles of pinecones, empty nests, and shreds of leather dispersed across the shop—but in an orderly fashion.

"Give me your map," he says, pointing to the scroll in one of my hands. I hand it over to him. He begins to trace the trails on smooth paper with his calloused fingers. I can't tell if his eyes are open; it's as if he's reading braille.

"Here," he says, his fingers stopping on a point. "This one will feel like it doesn't end. It's a tough, old trail, but it's the least crowded. And when it ends, you'll sure as hell know."

We thank him, and he retreats into his shop like an unencumbered bear. I look back over my shoulder one more time before I exit. He's using a small knife to carve the handle of something— another fly swatter, an eating utensil, maybe a hairbrush. Wood shavings flutter out of his hands to the floor.

An hour later, Ben and I are standing where the shopkeeper pointed on the map.

The wooden sign has chipped, white letters covered in hardened splotches of bird poop. It reads: "Ramsey Cascade Falls 4.0 miles".

Last night, the cicadas pulsed louder than our combined voices at max volume. They shook like hundreds of maracas inside our chests. Though we couldn't hear any as we began the trail, I swear it felt like they were watching us from their hiding spots in the trees.

The breeze carries a light mist, so I pull on my hood. Ben tightens the straps of his new backpack. "Trust me, Sarah. I used to be a Boy Scout," he'd said, the first time he tried it on in our living room weeks ago.

I squeeze Ben's hand as we trudge through the wet dirt, which begins to harden as we reach the places where the earth juts out. The grass splits, making the edge of the mountain look like it has sideburns.

Ben spots wild turkeys—a mother and two babies. The mother's fatty wattles jiggle as she huddles her babies close, quickly escorting them away from Ben, who's running at them like a crazed puppy, his backpack bouncing behind him.

I can't take my eyes off the ground. Knobby vines crisscross in the dirt, dipping in and out of palettes of freckled stones. I pick up a flat stone that looks like it's been splattered with paint and hand it to Ben. He rubs his thumb over it before slipping it into his pocket. I think of the sleepy shopkeeper, picking up his favorite things and slipping them into his pockets.

Thin brooks gape like scars between rocks. We spy bright yellow fungi, flickering in the weeds, water spiders moonwalking on water, a muddy gecko resting on a boulder.

We read a sign that described an incident where a couple of hikers had carelessly left food on this trail. It attracted a bear, and rangers were forced to shoot the bear because it would've attacked people. I wonder if the ground shook when the enormous, brown mass collapsed to the ground. We kill the bear, then put its face on novelty items we buy from the gift shop.

Water surges beyond the rock walls, calling to us. The trail gets steeper, forcing me to grab at branches, roots, and clumpy ledges for balance. I use them to propel my body forward. I can feel a tugging in the back of my calves. Drops of sweat dot Ben's forehead.

This becomes the pattern. We climb and climb until little pools of water greet us. We're careful not to stumble over the slimy rocks when we dip our hands into the cool water. Ben cups his hands to fill them and splashes water onto his face. I scan it to see if he looks younger. He doesn't look much different from when I met him seven years ago— when he sat behind me in math class, too shy to even ask me to borrow a pencil.

We lean against thick trunks that stoop over crumbly, pie crust edges. The trees all seem to look down, so we follow their gaze. They're looking at the falls. Each fall is a strand, and together they blend into a streaming head of hair. (Mountains have long hair!)

"Hey, um, I need you to know this is the closest I have ever felt to you," I tell Ben.

I feel strong. Look at me climb. See my hands grab hunks of dirt. See my legs propel me higher. Climbing is intimacy—like a virginity I didn't know I had until I lost it.

Please let me carry these feelings with me when I go to work, reignite them when I'm miserable in traffic. When I feel alone at my desk or even with a crowd of people. I will remember.

The longer we climb, the louder we whine. We pout with fat lips like kids in the backseat of a car and drag our heavy limbs along. There's a pounding that sounds like watered-down thunder. This must be the end. We hobble like turkeys up the last set of steps to see what is on the other side of the colossal rock.

And there she is—the mother of all waterfalls, spilling from every pore of the jagged rock. I can't tell where each fall begins and ends; they're braided together. The beads of water bounce from one rock to the next, spraying our faces. My bottom lip trembles.

Ben and I cross the slippery platform. He suddenly loses his footing and plops down in the base of the large waterfall. I gasp, terrified the current will sweep him away over the top of the falls, all the way down from where we first began to climb. The falls at the base of the mama waterfall are even more treacherous. They drop soundlessly, but with violence.

Ben stands up and brushes himself off. I huddle close to him, sigh with relief.

A family snaps photographs near the falls. We watch them grinning like children on their first day of school. One of the little boys is wearing swim trunks. He has collected stones and stacked them.

Ben says something, but I don't hear it. His voice sounds like a whisper reserved for someone else.

Ben and I reach our timid hands out to greet the waterfall. It has a handshake that rattles through our entire bodies.

Someday if I have a kid, I will tell them I met the famous Ramsey Cascade Falls.

SHADES OF NUDE

In my gym's locker room, I watch a woman. She's there every Tuesday at the same time. I'll be straightening my hair in the mirror, putting myself together for work, and suddenly she'll be bent over between the lockers slathering lotion between her toes.

The first time I saw her take off all her clothes, I immediately throttled my gaze down to my phone, blinking on the long countertop below the mirror. *Did I miss a call?* I thought. I squinted and pretended to focus my attention.

I looked up.

She was taking long strides on the thin carpet. Her auburn mane freshly showered, shaking its excess drops off like a wet animal coming inside from the rain. *What is this, a nude beach?* I scoffed.

192

But now, I can't help but admire her. I pass by her, and sometimes we even exchange hellos in a daily grind kind of way. I've come to expect her oblivious nakedness.

Really I just like that she lotions her toes. She even lotions the folds underneath each breast. She does it precisely, like she's checking for lumps. Before she arrives, I shed my damp clothes underneath my towel. I let them fall into a heap on the floor, then shimmy into my clean ones. The towel doesn't completely cover my body. There's always a pie slice of skin exposed between the two ends. I utter a silent curse to the establishment for not providing towels large enough to cover my entire body. I could bring one from home. Maybe I like the self-torture.

I slither out of my sports bra while replacing it with the one I wear for daily use. It used to be a soft, baby blue, but now a little brown leaks through, like a stain on a soiled diaper. I swap bras in a quick 1-2-3 maneuver. I've gotten pretty skilled at it. I'm like the Spiderwoman of whipping off bras.

A few times, someone has had a locker right next to mine. I'll let out an inaudible sigh, again cursing the establishment for assigning this poor soul a place on top of mine. The other woman and I avoid eye contact and trade clunky apologies for being in each other's way. In trying to avoid each other, we almost knock heads.

Sometimes I wait until she's gone. I'll busy myself with tasks inside my purse or on my phone to make it look like I put my dressing on hold for more pressing things. If I'm idling long enough, I'll excuse myself to the bathroom stall and change in there. Who knew getting dressed could be such a hassle?

But back to the naked woman.

She applies lipstick. She scratches at blackheads. She plucks her eyebrows. Sometimes she stretches. I wonder if, after her workout, she completely bypasses the cool down area lined with blue mats just outside the locker room. Instead she opens up her fingers wide as peacock wings in the middle of the locker room. She curls her spine, bowing her chin deep against her chest. It's like she's waking up, and this is her first stretch of the morning.

If I were to guess, I'd say she's about fifty. Her skin is the rugged mountain terrain she has explored and survived. It has little luster left. There's an extra knob of flesh on one shoulder, a faint whisper of a scar on her right hip. I've noticed the random patches of freckles on her back. They're scattered like clusters of stars. I wonder if anyone has named them. Her toenails are trimmed, but never painted. Her stomach protrudes, and there are slivers of pink sketched into her hips.

Maybe she's birthed a kid or two. Maybe she's lost a lot of weight and has a triumphant weight loss story to tell. She has conquered something. With some people, you can just tell.

Who else aside from me has marveled over this body? Maybe she's been in and out of every relationship in the book—the pulsating one dipped in sweat and tangled hair, the one that's as comfortable as morning coffee and as unapologetic as peeing with the bathroom door open, the one with brooding backdrops and as codependent as sharing needles. The one where she had to fight to be herself. Maybe she shared a bed for many years with the same person. Maybe she's held a hand or two through coughing fits that ended in death.

Maybe she's alone by choice. Maybe her favorite relationship is the one where she slips in and out of herself and tries each part of her life on for size. She routinely needs to be fitted because she keeps shrinking and expanding.

I've never been one of those people who can spend long periods of time naked. I find it nearly impossible to sleep in that state. I'll wake up every hour and shiver, even if I'm not cold. When the slumber wears off, I'm ashamed. I feel like I need to explain myself.

More recently, though, I've started to try some daily routines without clothes. I've quickly realized my favorite thing to do naked is eat a bowl of cereal in my bed.

I sit with my shoulders hunched and my belly and bowl resting in my lap. I imagine pregnant women get these moments. They caress their full stomachs. I caress my breakfast and stare at my own life between my knees.

I do jumping jacks in my living room until my chest is on fire.

My thighs make harsh slapping sounds when they unite at my body's equator. My tits feel stretched as dusty rubber bands. I want to scratch them as they begin to itch. The rubbing spreads warmth between my legs. For a second, I wonder if anyone has ever climaxed while doing vigorous exercise. Did this person fall down in sheer ecstasy?

I hack away at some half-finished document on the computer.

All I'm missing is a trail of smoke descending from a lit cigarette. Ah, there it is. After each puff, I feel a little more grandiose. What if Da Vinci's plump ladies came to life and decided to write about him? I drop the act and forget myself. I smile at the sentence I just wrote. It's not bad. At least it's there. And I mean it.

I laugh my ass off over some comedy bit I find on Netflix.

I'm proud that I can laugh without clothes, and not necessarily at myself. There's plenty of jiggling involved. The soft fat behind my biceps, the rolls on my stomach, the skin around my throat, my earlobes—they all ripple like water touched by stones. Each stone is another pitch in my wide range of laughter. I place my hand on my heart and laugh. My skin was made for this. Raw bodies don't always lead to orgasms, but they can if they want to.

During one of my experiments, my boyfriend arrives home from work early. I stand frozen in the middle of our living room. I'm in the middle of a move that looks like a drunken Macarena.

He throws his heavy backpack on the table and scratches his beard. He's had a long day. Naturally, he thinks I'm a surprise for him.

He asks me why I have to be a tease. Playful banter. Not this time. I laugh. I check for signs of hurt.

"Why does my nakedness always have to be for you?"

"Touché," he says.

This time I'm the naked woman in the locker room. I suck in my stomach. I feel like I'm being watched and assessed even though I'm alone. It's like the lockers are bursting with secrets to tell each other. The benches cough in between hushed judgments about my chafed bikini line. I hear a rustle a few rows down. I tear at my gym bag. The zipper won't unzip fast enough. My heart is a ping-pong ball inside my chest.

I look up, and I'm peering into the face of a young girl. She has thick, red spirals of hair, and she's cradling an orange backpack covered in patches as prominent and proud as bumper stickers. I forget why I'm here at all. At any point now, this girl will convey she's uncomfortable in one movement. She will silence me with her eyes. She will shun me, stepping over my nakedness like it's a puddle she's not about to step in.

Wait for it.

She says, "Hey, aren't you that girl from my Friday morning spin?"

"Oh, yeah," I stutter. I stand up straighter.

"Cool. The last one kicked my ass. It felt like we were out of the saddle the entire time."

"It really did. I thought it would never end."

"Right? We did it, though. See you Friday."

I watch her turn the corner, exiting the locker room. I wonder what she has inside her backpack aside from clothes. If these items come close to explaining her. I wonder, when she strips down to the bare minimum, what she will feel.

I lift a fresh shirt from my half-open gym bag. My clothes smell of Downy April Fresh fabric softener. It doesn't smell so much like rain, but I like it anyway. I rub the shirt against my face. Cotton to skin. I run my fingers along my lips. I taste like salt. Skin to skin.

DA BOSS

My dad calls me while I'm in the middle of drawing a robin with a top hat. I'm sitting in my office at my desk, which is covered in pencils and shreds of eraser. There is a permanent water stain fading into its fake wood. My favorite tree outside my two-story window just started flowering, and I can't wait to watch its seashell petals open up in the sun.

"Can you bring your grandmother a blanket?" he asks. "I'm at work, and my hands are tied at the moment."

"A blanket?"

"Yes, a blanket. She spilled something all over the one she has. Orange juice, I think."

"It's no problem," I say. "Hey, you holding up?"

"Don't even get me started," he laughs, and then it's silent. For a second I think we've disconnected, until he clears his throat and tells me goodbye.

I took off work the day I found out my grandmother was dying from pancreatic cancer. I needed to be near her.

When I visited her, I fumbled for words to say. It was hard to see such a busy body restless in a hospital bed. My grandmother—who had been a caretaker for most of her life—had raised her siblings, her children, and even some of her grandchildren.

I shade the robin's breast, trying not to lean into the dark parts and smear the drawing with my fists.

My friend from Georgia asked me if I wanted to make anything for the store that's just opened up on the farm where she works. She's making homemade kombucha and coasters. I asked her if I could draw animals in peculiar ways and turn them into prints, and she was delighted. Sometimes she sends me pictures of the farm animals. I drew Brownie the goat licking an ice cream cone last week.

I'm grateful to have this weekend outlet to keep my mind off impending death and work. Work at the magazine has been stressful. Another one of our editors quit, and it's less about the extra work and more about the loss of a friend who speaks the same nine-to-five dysfunction as you.

My dog sleeps on the ground next to my feet. She kicks her legs, and I place my hand on her side to calm her.

Getting a puppy a few weeks ago came in handy. Maya is some kind of beagle on stilts I named after Maya Angelou. When she stands, she's as tall as me. She's a decent fly killer and an expert cuddler. I adore the warm weight of her, curling into the crevices of my legs. I pack us both into layers of blanket until we're one large sushi roll.

My grandmother scared me when I was growing up. I assumed that she didn't really like us all that much because she left for Bingo whenever we came over. She'd scribble strict notes in all caps like SHOES OFF IN THE HOUSE. DON'T TOUCH THIS BUTTON. CASSEROLE IN FRIDGE.

RINSE DISHES IN SINK. She signed them all as
DA BOSS.

My grandpa spoiled us in her absence. We'd
hunch over TV dinner trays, polish off one of his
famous triple-decker turkey sandwiches, and be
glued to some show on Nickelodeon by the time she
returned. The second we heard her key click in the
door, my siblings and I ripped our feet off the
couch, quickly swept crumbs off the table.

The first thing she did when she came home was
hang up her hat and fluff her blonde wig in the
mirror. We were silent as mice as she heated up
soup or joined us in the living room with a bowl of
fruit she'd lay out on the table for everyone.

"Eat," she'd say, even though we'd been
stuffing our faces all afternoon.

She'd offer her cheek out for each of us to kiss.
Doctors were amazed at how mobile she was, how
nimble she was, despite a lifetime of various
arthritis-related surgeries. Her skin was creamy and
soft, but underneath that were layers of elephant
hide.

204

She gave the kind of criticism that seared like a bee sting. Things that annoyed her ranged from the following: our clothing choices, spending habits, tattoos, loudness, and long hair that she hated having to pluck off the carpet.

"Stop picking your fingers," she'd tell me. "Or you're gonna get an infection, and the doctor will need to amputate."

Once, my older sister told me this story about my grandmother at a casino. She was waiting in line to use the pay phone, and the woman in front of her was taking too long for her liking. My grandmother asked the woman how much longer she was going to be.

"Lady, just calm the hell down," the woman scolded.

My grandma struck her across the face with the back of her hand. She showed her affection through food and gifts. Like her spirit lived in the golden candlestick holders that belonged to her mother. It took me a while to understand her love language— that took the form of helping my sister open her first checking account, and introducing me to her gynecologist.

Don't get me started on her meatballs. The secret ingredient is veal, which bothered me when I figured out that veal was baby cow, but didn't prevent me from relishing every last bite. I can still picture her with her sleeves rolled up, massaging egg, garlic, and seasoning into the raw meat. And I can see the candied happiness that welled up in her eyes when everyone sat around the table for Christmas dinner.

Her home was always a cozy seventy-one degrees, and the blankets she kept in a wicker basket next to the couch always smelled like her. Pictures of Italians lined the walls. The Sicilian side of the family had olive-colored skin and frowned in their photos. They all wore dirt on their faces and their foreheads glistened with sweat—like they had been working in the sun all day.

My favorite photo of my grandparents is one of them on their wedding day. My grandmother was only eighteen when she married my grandfather.

She wore a scared but happy expression on her round, glass doll face. Small, chocolate eyes and full, pink lips. Everyone called her Dolly. My grandfather wore a goofy, just-won-the-jackpot kind of smile.

Her mother had only been fourteen when she had her. Her grandparents moved to the U.S. from "some little hick town" in Sicily. Her grandfather was in the U.S. for twelve years before he sent for his family, who had become strangers to him by then.

My grandmother can't remember many instances when her parents weren't fighting. Her mother, who had rushed into a relationship with her father to flee a tumultuous home life, eventually had a nervous breakdown. When she stabbed my grandmother in the arm with a fork, that had been the last straw. While her mother was hospitalized, my grandma looked after her younger sister, who was twelve years younger than she was. It took many years, but eventually mother and daughters found their way back to each other and were able to heal their relationship.

My grandma and I have gotten closer since my grandpa's death. She texts me when she can't sleep, sends me coupons and birthday cards, even if they're addressed to other people. The last time I visited her at her apartment in an assisted living community, we watched *Family Feud* together.

"That Steve Harvey is a great host," she said.

My grandfather knew how to love my grandmother in the right ways—through space and acts of service like scrubbing the kitchen floor on his hands and knees. Though they slept in separate rooms, the walls a barrier against my grandfather's snores of thunder, they came together for the weather reports and old films they remembered growing up.

I will never forget the sight of my grandmother massaging lotion into my grandfather's feet three days before he died.

Now she tears up every time anyone so much mentions my grandpa's name. "He gave me sixty-three beautiful years," she sniffled, as I took her hand. It's small like mine.

The next time I visit my grandma in the hospital, she's ordering tilapia off a menu. Her glasses sit on the edge of her nose. Her hair is matted down, but her color is rosy today, not the dusty gray that I noticed during our first visit.

"Do you have any mashed potatoes?" she asks over the phone. She sees me, smiles, and holds up a finger. "How about gravy? Uh-huh. The brown kind?"

She reminds them that she has ice cream in the freezer that my dad got her (Ben and Jerry's vanilla) that she's saving for later.

My grandma says the nurses keep coming in like it's a "damn three-ring circus". As she says this, a nurse appears in the doorway. Her sneakers squeak on the floor as she enters the room. She's young and has thick bangs and buggy eyes. She talks really slow to my grandmother, who's deaf in one ear.

"Dolly. Would. You. Like. Me. To. Raise. This. Table?" she asks.

My grandmother rolls her eyes and says, "Hunny, I'm deaf, not stupid." I laugh uncomfortably.

Another nurse comes in. She's thin and fidgety. Her hair is tied into a fishtail braid. She and my grandmother exchange a look that insinuates that they both know what time it is.

"If you're giving me another one of those pills, I don't want it. They make me gassy," my grandmother tells her.

The nurse laughs when my grandmother refuses the Ensure shake on her tray, which she says tastes like chalk and asks for her ice cream instead. They shuffle slowly to the bathroom together. My grandmother clings to the nurse's arm. The nurse takes her time with her, which makes my heart surge with gratitude. The back of my grandma's gown flutters open, and she wrenches it closed. I've never seen this much of her skin before.

When she settles back into bed, I show my grandmother a post on Facebook that my sister wrote when she first learned of my grandmother's diagnosis. They haven't spoken to each other for a year. It all started when my sister lost her job waiting tables and stopped making payments on her car, which was under my grandmother's name.

The women in my family carry grudges in the pits of their stomachs. Sometimes, they forget why they're mad. My grandmother never forgets anything. But instant forgiveness sweeps over her face as she reads the post. It explains that our grandparents practically raised her, and she's devastated to hear the news of my grandmother's cancer.

"We raised her like she was our own kid," Grandma wails. I hand her a tissue and stroke her arm.

My dad appears in the doorway. His jeans are stained and torn at the knees, and he's wearing a Cubs hat that's not all the way on his head. He looks worried. He brushes his eyebrow and stares off into the distance.

He walks over to us and puts a hand on my shoulder. I concentrate on the warmth of it.

"How are you doing, Bear?" he asks me.

My dad sinks into the chair opposite of my grandmother. We're all silent for a while until my dad starts telling a story. He tells inappropriate stories when he's nervous. He recalls the one about how my grandmother made him get a vasectomy after my brother was born. She was the first to say something when my dad told everyone he was going to have another child she believed he couldn't afford.

"Ma grabbed me by the ear and took me to 'Dr. Snip Snip'," he says, sucking in his spit and making the sound of snipping. He slices the air with his fingers, like they're a pair of scissors.

"Dad, no offense, but I'm not interested in hearing about your balls," I say.

My grandmother chimes in. "I remember your grandfather's vasectomy. He was so worried that his thing no longer worked," she says, smiling devilishly. "It worked just fine when we tested it out. He gave me 'twinkle eyes', and I knew we were good to go."

I feel like I'm going to throw up. Being back in the heart of my family's drama has always made my body respond in subtle ways. My mind searches for an escape, briefly wandering back to my office, where I can be alone and press graphite into paper.

My grandma asks me about work, and I show her a copy of an article I wrote. She is proud. So is my dad. I've lost track of the amount of these things I've cobbled together, and this is the first time I've shown anyone in my family my professional work.

I think about the poems my younger sister and I wrote for my grandfather that my grandmother framed and hung in their old kitchen. My poem was flowery and long-winded and my sister's was short, clunky, and sweet.

I never lost my affinity for words, but I certainly stopped sharing them with the people I love. I've realized that as you get older, love gets scarier.

I suddenly want to show them all the things. I show them a picture of the robin drawing. I show them pictures of my dog. They have respect for me now that I'm taking care of something. It's not a kid, but it's just as good, they both assure me. It surprises me how accepting they are.

My grandmother asks me, "Is there anything you can't do?"

CRAP APPLES

I needed more paper towels. My boyfriend and I woke at three a.m. to the sound of our dog Maya squirting onto the carpet. I had a feeling the rotten crab apples she had vacuumed up during our walks would catch up to her, but I was hoping it would cause less of a crime scene.

Ben untangled himself from our bed and escorted a somber Maya to the back door, her long ears sagging to the ground. I stumbled around the house in a half-awake stupor, looking for something I could use to clean the mess, only to discover a paper towel roll with one sheet left. I sacrificed one of our older dishtowels—one with a strawberry pattern—sprayed the last three drops of carpet cleaner onto it, and scrubbed the carpet in feverish circles.

This is not what people have in mind when they adopt puppies. Most viral videos depict an ecstatic adult drowning in a sea of fuzzy ears and stubby tails. A man rolls around with ten Goldendoodles that lick his face and tug his shoelaces. What joy. No one watches videos where one puppy takes a dump that another puppy consumes.

It's morning, and the kitchen swims around me. I open a cabinet door and discover we don't have coffee filters. I can feel my ears begin to burn. What the hell do I do when I'm at the store?

"We need a Costco membership," I say.

Maya jumps and extends her long front legs onto the counter.

"Get the fuck down!" I yell.

Ben says, "Okay, but do you remember our last trip to Costco?"

I stare at Ben and wait for him to refresh my memory. The collar of his work shirt is stained with toothpaste, and his hair is matted to one side of his head. He's one of those people who plays video games until midnight, then slips into his clothes and out the door in less than ten minutes every morning. In the time we've lived together, I recall seeing him look in a mirror only a handful of times.

"You said Costco was 'overrated', remember? You were most impressed with the onion dispenser."

"That was a damn good hotdog."

"If you want a Costco membership, let's get one. I have to go, though. Love you."

Ben plants a sloppy kiss on my forehead, and I stifle the urge to wipe it off.

"Love you, too," I say.

"Be safe," he says.

"Thanks, Dad," I say in the mousey voice I use to tell Maya that Ben's home. We've become the nauseating set of pet parents who can't decide between a bumblebee or a ladybug outfit to stuff their fur child into for Halloween.

Maya and I stare impatiently at each other. Her mouth is agape, and her tootsie roll eyes look like they're about to melt right off her face. She's part hound, so her sadness droops extra low. She looks like she's trying to explain to me the unfortunate predicament she's in. Two weeks ago she was in a similar one. She'd stolen and devoured an entire bag of grapes, and I had to take her to the vet to get her stomach pumped. There's still charcoal stains on her pink collar.

I pity Maya. She can't help it. Some dogs literally eat themselves to death. What a sick world we live in where dogs can OD on grapes.

Maya scrapes her paws against my back, protesting my trip to the drug store. While I'm at the store, I buy an eight-pack of paper towels, carpet cleaner, and a grass-fed beef bone to make up for leaving her behind. She's probably making it rain in the kitchen at this very moment.

I carry the paper towels in my arms; the plastic packaging rubs against my chin. It's a sunny fall day in suburbia. Lawns are trimmed and leaf-free, but littered with goose shit that Maya likes to eat. Cars whir in all directions. Drivers who pass me stare at me with long faces, probably wondering why I'm not at work.

I feel a buzz in my back pocket. I place the paper towels on the ground with the rest of the items on top of it and reach for my phone. My coworker wants to know why I forgot to run someone's article last month. I offer her no explanation and tell her we'll run it next month.

I hear a rustling of leaves. There's a man walking behind me about fifty feet away. White, middle-aged, feathery hair that glows in the sun. He has his hands in his pockets and walks leisurely. I pick up my items and cross the intersection.

About a block away from my house, a silver Honda rockets to the side of the road next to me. It lets out a perturbed honk. The driver is a black woman with a shimmery purple cloth bundled on her head.

"Do you need a ride?" she asks me through her window. The whites of her eyes bulge.

"Uhh, no. Thanks though," I tell her slowly.

Then she points one red nail at the man walking down the street behind me. "Do you know this man?"

219

He and I exchange baffled looks—then he squints up at the sky, and I back at the woman.

"No, I don't know him," I tell her.

"Are you sure you don't need a ride, then?"

"Thank you, but no. I really appreciate the gesture. I live just down the block," I tell her.

"Okay… well, stay safe."

The woman's eyes linger on my face for a while, like she'll need to remember it for later. Then she watches the man, who's now made it all the way down the block past my house. He's whistling.

I smile to reassure her. A stranger has never cared this much about my safety.

I'm relieved to find Maya curled up on her bed in the kitchen. Nothing has been soiled or destroyed.

She's happy to see me until she notices the plastic bag in my hand. She thrusts her long snout into the bag, and I push her back.

"Maya, sit," I say in my sternest voice.

After squirreling her ass around, she sits it down, not exactly touching the ground, more levitating slightly above it. Her mouth is agape again, and she's silently urging me to produce what's rightfully hers. She nods her head with exaggerated goodness.

I place the bone in her wet jaws, and she bites down. She drops it to the floor and bats it between her paws.

In the three months I've known Maya, I've learned that she is the perfect fit for chasms. Like the one that grows in bed between two people as night takes them. The world is sane and secure when she's nestled in the small of my back or adding to the warmth between my legs. Though different in my waking hours, I still find it easier to slip into uncharted realms of possibility with a companion who has blind, stupid trust in me. Dogs are believers.

I stare out our sliding door, past the abstract wet-nose paintings on the glass. I glare at the crab apple tree, which splits down the middle and veers off into two directions. Bees bounce back and forth from its fallen spawn, rotting in the grass.

There are several deflated crab apples scattered across our patio that will surely lead Maya to temptation. I reach for the broom behind my fridge and crack open the sliding door. Maya watches me as I sweep the red beasts into the grass.

When I turn back around, her face is gone. I slide open the door.

"Maya?" I call, but there is no sound of limbs skidding across the floor.

"Maya?" I call again, shoving a couch and peering behind it.

My attention turns to the door, which is still open. Panic jolts inside my chest, as my brain formulates scenarios: screeching wheels and a lifeless Maya in the middle of the road.

I race outside. There's a child swinging on a swing in the park across the street. He's wearing light-up shoes. I recognize him. His name is Om, the sound that people make when they're meditating, which I could use a little of right now.

A few weeks ago, Om had popped his head over the brick wall surrounding our house and introduced

222

himself to Maya, who I had to wrestle down so he could pat on the head. Om and Maya have become fast friends. He waits in the same spot for me to return from work every day and take Maya out for our walk.

"Where's my friend?" he asks me as I approach him. His heels touch the wood chips, and the lights play tag in his shoes.

"I don't know, actually. I was hoping you had seen her run past here?"

"Oh no! Maya's lost?" His eyes bulge and forehead creases. He looks adult-like in his fear.

"I think she may have escaped out the back door," I tell him. "Will you please come find me if you see her?"

Om nods his head dutifully, a silent salute.

A brisk walk turns into a sprint, which turns into a brisk walk. I circle the next block and the next. Lawn gnomes mock me with jolly smiles. Geese hiss. A bored yellow lab sits in a driveway unattended, warming in the sun. No one can help me.

I think about calling Ben, but don't want him to electrocute himself while he's wiring a panel. That and I don't want the sound of my own terror to be reflected back to me. It was Ben's idea to get this dog, I think, wanting to free myself from all blame.

I decide to stand on top of a baseball mound for elevation. I peer around a dewy field and there, in the bowl of it, is a man. He's wearing a plaid button-up; it's open, exposing a large gut. His hair glows. It's the same man from this morning.

At the man's foot is a soft pile of fur with a cowhide pattern, like Maya. The pile isn't moving. The man begins to let out a low scratchy laugh that sounds like metal scraping against the pavement, and I begin to sprint toward him. I've never fought another person, let alone a man before, but the adrenaline propels me forward, and my fists tighten and burn.

"Get the hell away from my dog!" I scream.

"Pardon?" he asks, peering down at me.

"What did you do to her?" I don't recognize my high-pitched, needlepoint voice. I feel like I'm drowning in the man's eyes, blue as swimming pools.

Maya springs from the grass and lunges at me. Her tail whips around. She licks my still-clenched fists.

"Is this your dog? I saw her running and called her over to me. She really likes having her tummy pet," he giggles.

"Uh, yeah…" I say. I'm slightly taken aback because I have never heard a grown man giggle or use the word 'tummy' in a sentence.

"What's her name?"

"Maya."

"Oh, Maya is a pretty name."

Maya nudges the man's hand. He scratches behind her ear, and she squints in contentment.

He says to her, "I bet you'd like to go home with your mom now, wouldn't you, Maya?" Her tail smacks the grass.

The knots in my chest loosen. I tell him, "Yeah, it's been an eventful morning. She ate all these crab apples and got sick. And then she takes off."

"Poor baby. Boil some chicken and rice for her. Serve it plain. Skip the dog food," he tells me. "My old dog, Sadie, she loved crab apples too. Err… she still loves them, I'm sure. I haven't seen her in a while. My wife took her when she left."

I wonder if the five o'clock shadow and grease stains are indicators that his wife left him more recently, but I don't want to ask anything about his personal life.

"Okay, well, thanks for calling her over to you. I appreciate it," I tell him, grabbing Maya by the harness.

"Maybe I can play with her again, sometime? If we run into each other again?" he asks.

"Sure," I laugh.

The man smiles. I think about Om peering over my brick wall with his toothless grin, asking to pet Maya. It's the same face.

LITTLE WOOD-SATYR

Word must have gotten out about Matthiessen State Park, because it's packed with people. Families pour out of minivans. Dogs choke themselves on their leashes. Young lovers grab each other's hands, ready, and tilt their bewitched faces toward the sun, their smartphones locked and loaded to snap photos of each other in front of ancient rock formations.

Mom says she regrets not bringing her handicapped placard, which doesn't matter because the questionable grassy knoll parking spots are all unmarked.

My mind wanders back to Walmart parking lots, to the Jewels and Chase Banks, and I remember people's faces, contorted with confusion and a pinch of anger when they saw my beautiful mother step out of the dusty Chrysler she had just maneuvered into a handicapped spot.

Sometimes she'd clear the air for the onlookers. "I have MS," she'd tell them with a peculiar confidence. They'd look down to the pavement and quickly shuffle inside the store.

Mom slips into her jet blue cooling vest and packs two chocolate Ensure shakes in the small satchel she's loaded up for our day trip. She peels open a package of trail mix and shakily pours it into her palm.

"My blood sugar is just a little low," she says, popping a handful of the mix into her mouth. "But you will be proud of me. I've been working out five days a week. I do hot yoga now."

I am proud of her. I'm proud of myself too as I slather my skin with sunscreen. I haven't lost my cool with her once. There's a part of me that suspects that the peace I feel oozing inside me is a sign. Maybe I have finally shed the chafed, half-dangling skin of my childhood. And the newest layer has no expectations for my mother. We're both excited, our faces drenched in sun.

There are dozens of stairs leading to the lower portion of the state park. She descends them slowly, her body nursing the railing. Years ago, her taking her time in front of a lot of people would have made my face hot. But now I wait patiently for her at the bottom of the stairs and smile up at her.

Muffled singing streams out from the clip-on speaker she's attached to her pants. I'm grateful for the background noise. I'm slightly more anxious when there isn't music playing.

Spotify recently notified me via email that I'd listened to over 76,000 minutes of music over the course of the year. The way some people grew up with television in the background is the way I grew up with music.

Since I called off my engagement and moved out, I've been listening to even more music than ever before. I think about my bare apartment with its heavy, hard to open doors and thin walls. The hospital bed that my stepmother's father was supposed to pass away in, but didn't, because he preferred his rocking chair.

Somehow I managed to create a new life for myself in a week. I told everyone in our Monday meeting that I didn't want to get married and wanted to live alone. It wasn't a shock to anyone. My boss let me stay on a blow-up mattress in her dogs' spare room for a few days while I searched for an apartment. Totally normal.

I was really excited about this recently updated number on the first floor near Roger's Park. I took my best friend with me, and everything checked out until she stepped on what appeared to be an adorable baby roach. So I bypassed my first crack at the city for an apartment in the suburbs that's five minutes away from my workplace.

It's hard to say for sure how I feel right now. I'm just getting used to my surroundings. I don't own a TV, and don't intend to for as long as I can stand the sound of my own thoughts.

There are mothers and daughters on every trail. It's easy to pick them out. An unspoken doting and a slight embarrassment is recognizable on the face of a freckled teenager. A yearning to be young again, cool again, is radiating from the chest of every mother.

How I used to loathe the sight of mothers and daughters. Mothers who tell their daughters to wait for them at the end of sidewalks. Little girls skipping to the tune of a million questions their mothers can't answer fast enough.

I remember a conversation between a mother and daughter walking out of a nail salon. The daughter blew on her silky new stubs. "Don't even bother putting your seatbelt on," the mother told her as they stepped inside their vehicle. Beauty over safety, sweetheart. The sentiment infuriated me. I dissected this mom like all the rest.

The air smells damp and mossy, and every stump has its own lacy layer of spiderwebs. I peer into a few tree holes, expecting to be greeted by a pair of shiny, shy eyes.

"What's the name of this song, Mom?"

"Silver Springs. Fleetwood Mac. It was my favorite for a while," she says.

"I've never heard this one before."

"It got me through the split with your dad."

These are the footnotes my mom has left at the end of her sentences for as long as I can remember. They are one of many reasons I haven't been able to be in the same space with her for more than thirty minutes without feeling a wave of disembodied wariness, profound disappointment, or disgust bordering on nausea overtake me.

But, for some reason, among the uneven walls carpeted in green and speckled rock formations, I recognize my own curiosity, a thirst for my mother's stories I have tilted my head away from for years.

My mom recalls her dizzying love with the same girlish look every time.

"He was still married to his first wife when he proposed to me," she says. "I was so young. I must have been out of my mind."

"I miss him, though," she adds. "He seems to have mellowed over the years. He never stopped providing for you guys, you know?"

"I know."

My mom and I stop on the bridge to watch the water cascade down the gorge underneath us. It's hot, but there's a playful breeze. I close my eyes and lean into the feeling of wind sifting through my hair like a lover plucking a strand and slipping it behind my ear.

A brown butterfly opens and closes its wings on the bridge's stone railing. I hold my index finger to its feelers, and it helps itself onto the tip. It opens and closes its dusty wings to reveal orange polka dots with black rings around them, reminding me of many pairs of blinking eyes.

"Will you look at that!" Mom says.

I delicately place my new friend back on the railing, but it bursts into a frantic dance around my face. My mother and I squeal like piglets.

"It must like you!"

A few months ago, my sister asked me if I felt like a pressed butterfly. She'd called me while I was on a trip in Spain I thought would rejuvenate my relationship with Ben. She'd noticed my collection of dried-up wings, sealed behind glass.

"No, Lee, I don't feel like a fucking pressed butterfly. What does that even mean?" I asked her. Ever since she's been going to school for professional counseling, she's been asking me questions like this.

That summer, my favorite tree—the one just outside my window that I've drawn and written about—attracted a storm of butterflies. They tossed and toppled over one another. It was like leaves falling but never touching the ground. It must be thrilling to make love in the air.

I mourn the loss of my relationship, mostly its comfort and familiarity, but I miss that tree romantically. The white flowers in the spring. The crab apples in the fall that gave my dog the shits. The vacant nest I was hoping something would occupy, but nothing ever did.

My mother has to stop every half mile or so. Whenever she starts to lean a little far to either side, I ask her if she wants to rest. Her forehead glistens with sweat. She hums along, the saxophone pouring out of her radio. I spot a man with a panting corgi hanging from his backpack. An elderly couple passes us, clutching their walking sticks.

"Finally some nice weather," the woman says, and her partner nods.

With ease, I slip back into the amalgamation of roles I held for years, the ones I came to defy: my mother's caretaker, guardian, best friend, emotional support. Our eyes are the same, brown as mud, and they hold each other in hypnotic ways.

My sister and mother have been talking a lot over the phone lately, trying to reconcile, a process that I've only done on my own through introspection and written reflection. But my sister, who is much braver than me, craves accountability, which is something I doubt she'll ever receive. But it's not my place to tell her to stop trying when she believes that she's so close to a breakthrough with my mom.

While I was in Spain, my mother and sister hashed it out in my living room. It ended with my sister screaming an exorcism: "GET OUT!"

My mom fled to the hell from where she came.

"I mean, jeez, how many times does someone have to say I'm sorry?" she asks me. We rest on a fallen tree trunk, watching bubbles pop in the algae green bog.

"It's not my place to say. It's your relationship," I say, leaning against my faithful boundaries. After the final detangling from my mother, I built them from the bones of my old self. I layered them with new meat. They've served me well over the years.

The truth is that my mom has justified every action she's ever taken. It's how she has survived. And I don't know. Somehow, I don't know how to blame her anymore.

My mom takes a swig of her Ensure shake. She offers me some, but I shake my head. I watch another brown butterfly flutter from one stump to the next, thinking about how being out here with my mom feels like I'm coming home for the first time in years.

BIRDS THAT FLY AWAY

The first time we see her, she's playing behind glass, entertaining herself with her own reflection. A fury of green, yellow, and red feathers, she hops around on two twig legs and wrestles a silver bell tied to the end of a square mirror. The mirror has a mealy, grayish streak across it. She scales the exhibit and dangles from its ceiling on a single leg, looking like an overripe piece of fruit about to drop from a branch.

Ben had always wanted a bird, but I did not. I had enough parakeets growing up.

But, sure enough, there she was in the middle of Petco as I walked toward the register with a bag of pellets for our rabbit. I had never seen an entire circus contained in such a small body. The staff let us take her for a joyride on our shopping cart. She blinked a pair of crazed eyes and chirped at us.

We decided to call her Khaleesi—mother of conures, which are basically mini dragons.

Khaleesi woke us up one Sunday with a whole symphony. She sang songs we had never heard. Tender chirps, short clicks, and guttural screams. There could have been three birds in one cage. Ben and I lay in bed and listened from under the covers. We had no clue where she'd picked up the new dialects.

After the concert was over, we applauded her and awarded her tiny pancakes. Ben cooked human-sized flapjacks and added a single drop of batter to the frying pan. The bird perched on the back of a dining room chair, holding her prize with one foot. She pulled it apart with her beak. We all laughed. Her laugh sounded like it was made with a synthesizer. She peeked out of my hair, leaning into our jokes like a faithful sidekick.

One night she fell asleep in the cavern between my neck and shoulder. I woke up in a sweat, afraid that I'd crushed her. I held her in my palms. Her face was buried into her feathers, her wings tucked

239

tight as a bud. Her eyes popped open, and she climbed up my arm, her claws poking into my skin. Once again she sought refuge in her human nesting ground.

Ben called me on the phone the day she flew away.

I wouldn't have picked up the phone, but I read the words, *It's serious. Call me.*

For months, I had been telling Ben I wanted to end our relationship because I was in love with someone else. The day Ben called, I was in bed with someone else.

Daniel's sweat-kissed, bare leg touched mine. I smiled at the teeth marks on his neck.

I was struck by my own tenderness with Daniel. My body betrayed me, disarmed me. His expressive eyes wandered over my face, as he described its shadows to me. He said it looked like I wanted to punch someone, that the ends of my hair were daggers to slay him. While he was inside me, he asked me to tell him a story. I told him nothing, but all my limbs radiated truth.

My phone rang three different times before I caved to its urgency.

"I'm sorry, but I have to take this," I told him.

"I opened the window only a little bit, and the bird flew out." Ben's voice clawed through the phone.

I swallowed my silence, which was replaced by a trail of his heavy sobs.

"I'm so sorry," he said.

"It was an accident," I said, gulping down hot tears. I wanted to cradle him.

If it's anyone's fault, it's mine. I'm split down the middle. Half in, half out, I wanted to say.

"The universe is punishing us," I told Daniel when I got off the phone with Ben. "My bird was collateral."

"It only feels that way," he said, running his fingers over my thigh.

"I have to go," I said, even though I wanted to stay.

I always wanted to know Daniel, even though he hardly noticed me. We were in different circles, living separate lives, and then I dragged him into mine. I just wanted to be close to someone who spoke his mind and wore a pair of heavy eyes out in the open.

The morning after one of our first nights together, we sat in a booth and shared a plate piled high with salmon, cream cheese, and capers. Our waitress refilled our coffees. She had a dramatic pair of hands. I told her she should be on Broadway. Daniel stared at me, and when I couldn't take the weight of his silence any longer, I stacked the pink flesh onto my bagel. Fish stuck to my fingers.

"What are you thinking?" I asked him.

"I'm just counting the number of times we've eaten together."

"How many?"

"Ten."

When I called off the engagement with Ben, he pounded his fists on the dining room table. He had never expressed this amount of anger before. Ben and I had known each other since we were teenagers, and—for the first time since I'd known him—he looked ancient. I hated myself for bringing out the grayness on his face. But I bared my teeth, ready to defend my newfound relationship.

"You know you're fucking me over," Ben said, his eyes dripping like ice cubes at the bottom of a glass.

"I'm doing this for me, not to fuck you over. I just want to be with someone else."

The words rose like bile. My words were broken glass I swallowed that made the voice in the back of my throat sound so haggard. I saw myself in the reflection of our sliding glass door. My eyes were two hot coals burning. Jagged shadows sliced at my face, making me look like some kind of Frankenstein woman.

I don't consider it a privilege to be the first one to break a man with a strong back and calloused hands. This was the same person who'd once held his palms out and boosted me over the wall of my childhood.

"Do you think she'll come back?" I asked Daniel. I'm afraid to ask him if he believes in miracles. So I don't. I kiss him on the mouth hard, and we tell each other goodbye.

Three days later, Ben and I tape flyers to lampposts together. We drive to Petco and pin up her picture on a bulletin board with all the other wayward companions.

"Last seen on February 21. You can lure her to you with fruit or pizza crust. Will pay reward."

Weak smiles wobble on our faces like feeble apologies. Our loss is what we have left, what keeps us taped together. We drive from place to place in the cold. It's negative three degrees outside. My fingers throb. On the flyer is a picture and description of Khaleesi. She lights up the paper like a flame.

GOLF BALLS

My dad lives across the street from a 260-acre golf course. Every day, he rides his bike along the perimeter, pausing to check his neighbors' front yards for any stray balls.

He stores the golf balls he finds in a large planter that sits on the deck he built a few summers ago. When he shows me the planter, he reminds me of a proud bird standing in front of its masterpiece of a nest.

The balls are all different colors—neon green, highlighter-bright orange, robin's egg blue, grass-stained white. There has to be at least three hundred of them.

"Sundays are when the hacks are out. Come on, I'll show you," he says, inviting me on a ride to his next haul. I ask my stepmom if I can borrow her bike. She's in the middle of staining a wooden board in "Mary's Garden", the garden she dedicated to her mother who passed away from Alzheimer's a few years ago. She's making a welcome sign to put in the front yard, though she hasn't had very many visitors since the beginning of the pandemic.

She didn't have very many visitors before the pandemic, either, come to think of it. I'm one of the few people she tolerates, really. My dad tells me it's because I "play politics". I think what he means is that I was respectful and nonexistent as a ghost living in their house while I waited tables and commuted to college in the city for four years. I guess survival is political.

"You can use my bike," she says, glancing up from her handiwork. "Your father just bought me a new seat. He calls it 'the big butt seat'." She's wearing a mask with violets on it. Her tired eyes bulge like a toad's.

This is the same exhaustion I've seen on countless faces of people in stores and pharmacies since the plague began. Last week, she and her coworkers chanted the same phrase under the grocery store's sickly lights. "No, we don't have any more toilet paper," they told the hordes of panicked people, desperate to take comfort in their end of the world shits.

My parents own an electrical business together. I was technically the CEO of it for a short while, just until my dad was sure the union wouldn't hold his pension ransom for going out on his own. My dad handles the work and customers, while my stepmother manages the books. It's your standard working class, under-the-breath power struggle that has put a strain on many marriages. My dad likes to spend, and she's better with the word "no" more than anyone I know.

Their garage is exquisite. The shelves are arranged with surgical precision. Every wrench and drill has a proper place, and his drawers are labeled according to bit size. I wouldn't doubt that my dad leveled off every space on the wall where his larger equipment hangs like trophies.

He shimmies alongside his workbench and wheels out the bikes one by one. We mount our steeds and take off down the block. It's such a sweet summer day that I almost forget why I've confined myself to my apartment for months. And oh my, is that a lovely gust of wind tussling my hair?

I'm wearing jorts and my favorite t-shirt imprinted with the kids from *Stranger Things*—but just their heads. Eleven has a bloody nose. Will's head is upside-down. My dad is wearing fringy jorts, his favorite Cubs World Championship t-shirt, and Sox hat. I guess baseball is political, too.

When we climb the hilly blocks, he stands on his pedals, looking like a hip teen about to bust a wheelie. I can't remember the last time it's been just the two of us. The sidewalk is flat, which makes for a smooth ride. We pass the house with all the painted birdhouses, the house with a brown fence stained with a silhouette of soldier crouching down underneath an American flag.

My dad used to take my siblings and me for bike rides on his visitation weekends when we were kids. He'd strapped a booster seat on the back of his dusty ten-speed for my brother, who reminded me of a baby orangutan with his fuzzy hair blowing all over the place. My dad pedaled fast, and my sister and I pedaled frantically to keep up. Our legs got strong from chasing after him.

"You know I saw Ben got a promotion on Facebook," my dad yelled over his shoulder.

"Oh, he did?" I yelled back.

I know he did. That's not the only recent development in his life. Barely a week before I moved out, Ben swiped right on a big-breasted nurse. From her public posts about work and cats, she seems like she has a decent sense of humor. She proclaims to be a "horse girl." I showed a picture of her with a checkered stallion to my friend Heather, who grew up raising horses and riding them.

"Those aren't even real riding boots," she said, handing my phone back to me.

Who am I to say what is real or fake, though. I spent the duration of an adult relationship probing for a deep connection that I was hoping would show up before I stepped into a church and uttered words about "forever." Then again, it was my idea to get married in the first place. Ben went along with the engagement, guessing it was what I wanted. He went along with everything—neither for nor against anything.

"I know he was a little analog, and you're digital, but I liked him," my dad says.

The digital/analog analogy is one of the most recent dad-isms my father uses to oversimplify the human experience.

"I know, Dad, but I wish you would stop bringing him up. I've moved on," I say even though my brain is fossilized with eleven years' worth of birthdays, outdoor trips, and Netflix marathons with a person who rocked me in his arms when I'd forget who I was or was too afraid to reckon with my history.

The truth is I would have never left him if I knew this pandemic was going to happen. While everyone I know is hunkering down and holding onto loved ones, I'm trying to relearn myself in the greater context of a changing world—which in the end doesn't feel all that bad.

"Hold on, here we go," says my dad, swinging his leg over his bike. I watch him scurry across the street and dive into an unkempt lawn. He squints, holding a small, white ball to the sun, examining it, then dusting it off like it's a dinosaur bone. He stuffs it into his pocket.

He leads me down a gravel path that's guarded by sunflowers, which have always reminded me of nosey neighbors that lean too far into other people's conversations. Nature's silent judges.

I stare at the back of my dad's short, boxy frame, wondering what he was like when he was growing up, how he dealt with heartbreak. I'd be interested to sit in a room with the eighteen-year-old version of him who loved to rock out to Black Sabbath under hazy, marijuana-induced clouds.

The trail spits us out onto the street. I swoop over to the sidewalk, but my dad sticks to the middle of the road. He doesn't seem to notice the black SUV that swerves around us. I look up at the middle-aged man with a patchy beard in the driver's seat. He purses his lips to say something then resigns himself to a discontented headshake.

"Sarah, you'll be alright," he says, seemingly to himself more than me. "You're a mover and shaker like me."

My dad's been sober for over twenty years. Like a lot of alcoholics in need of a calling, he found another way to shock his system—hours of exhausting manual labor.

His body is full of metal parts: a replaced rotator cuff, mended knees, and now a Frankenstein foot that's been under the knife he forgets how many times.

He was wearing a boot on this foot when I first moved out into an apartment on my own. I remember him hobbling through the front door with his apprentice Luís, who helps my dad with everything from digging manholes to locating the missing bucket of tools he may or may not have left at a jobsite. They had been carrying a bookshelf my dad used for canned goods and Costco-sized jars of pasta sauce that he was now bequeathing to me.

I had been furiously typing up a blog for work—a nauseating number about a wedding held at one of the Newport Mansions. I looked up and thanked them both, then continued to type. My hair had been matted down with grease, and I was wearing a brace to nurse the carpal tunnel that was starting to develop in my right wrist.

It was that day I realized I was becoming my dad, and I needed to slow down in my life, that my body was clearly trying to tell me something. Sometimes people use what they love to do and turn it against themselves.

"Got a live one!" my dad says, hopping off his bike again and trotting towards a large patch of grass.

Just as he's about to collect his prize, a bald man wearing an army jacket throws his entire body onto the spot in the grass in front of my father's feet. He wrenches a ball from the earth, a clod of dirt wedged between his fingers. As he collects himself and straightens up, it's clear he's at least half a foot taller than my dad.

"This one is mine," he says in a gravelly voice with a slight Polish accent.

For a moment, I think I'm going to see my father go head-to-head with another grown man over a golf ball, and I'm wondering if now is the time to dial my stepmother.

This wouldn't be the first time in my life I've seen my dad charge down another man. Once he nearly kicked down the door of a forty-something-year-old neighbor who had asked a twelve-year-old me if he could hold my hand—to which I agreed reluctantly. They wrestled on the concrete in between our apartments' entryways until the guy surrendered with both hands raised. My dad spat on the ground and told him between labored breaths to keep his "filthy gorilla hands" off me.

My dad and the bald man stand planted in the grass, still and stoic as gargoyles. A bead of sweat drips down the man's head. My dad's open hands have morphed into fists.

"Hey, Dad," I say in a burly voice that I don't recognize. "Can we get back to our bike ride?"

His next move surprises me. He unfurls his fists, which are etched with a lifetime of wiry scars and says, "This one is yours." He leaves his opponent wordless in the grass and returns to his bike.

We bring our golf balls back to the planter. My dad dumps his five into the pile while I toss in two of my own finds. We stare into the pool of his summertime achievement. One day when he finally retires, he says, he'll take up golfing. Right after he moves to Tennessee and builds his countryside dream house.

Before I leave, I force a hug onto him. Even before social distancing, my dad has always been weird about hugs. "Squeeze tighter," I'd tell him when I was a kid, and then he'd squeeze so tight I thought my eyes would pop out of my head. This is the first hug I've had in over a month. He's soft and smells like the inside of his garage.

As I drive away, I turn my head to watch the golfers on the other side of the fence leisurely strolling across the immaculate green field. I picture my dad in his tattered jeans and cutoff shirt, moving in slow, long strides—happy, self-forgiving, and unfazed by time.

DIRTY THIRTY

It's my thirtieth birthday, and I'm enjoying a glass of champagne and my dog's unconditional love. We're hunkered down on the couch together. As she naps, she doesn't even notice when I roll her floppy ears into thin tortillas around my fingers.

I am newly single and a part-time dog owner. I share Maya with my ex. He let me have her early this week. This is the first birthday I've spent without him, without anyone at all.

The date is January 4, 2020. Six months ago, I was engaged to be married to Ben, my high school sweetheart.

The closer I got to marriage, the more I battled with my own intuition. For years it was telling me that I was ready for a different life. I knew deep down that life would be harder without him. It's true. Life is harder without him. That doesn't make me any less ready to find new ways to grow into my skin.

I wanted to venture down a nature trail with Maya earlier today, but I typed the wrong address into my GPS. Forty minutes out, three tolls later, I pulled up in front of a small children's park. The place I wanted to visit is forty minutes in the opposite direction.

I drove home, sinking into the defeat. My eyes caught the hawks leering from the top of streetlights, fat pigeons all huddled together, weighing down power lines.

"Sara" by Fleetwood Mac started playing from my Spotify shuffle playlist. My mom always liked this song. If you asked her, she might say I'm the poet in her heart. She named me Sarah not realizing it was one of the most popular names of 1990. Though, as a guy I once loved pointed out, I was "one of the first Sarahs of the 90s".

My mom actually named me after Sarah in the Bible. Sarah in the Bible loved to laugh. She basically spit in God's face when he told her she would have a baby with her husband Abraham at age ninety. She didn't believe him, so she coerced her husband into getting drunk and having sex with their handmaiden, Hagar. Both women got pregnant. Except Sarah then asked Abraham to banish Hagar and her baby, Ishmael.

If you ask me, it was pretty shitty what Sarah did. Swept the handmaiden under the rug. Muslims certainly seem to think so. While Sarah is a revered figure in the Christian scripture, Hagar is hailed in the Quran.

To my mom, the name Sarah was fitting. I was her very own miracle baby. To me, the term "miracle" is a lot to live up to. She tells me this story every birthday. I half listen. Generally, I find religious fervor to be overwhelming and sometimes straight manipulative. But this year I took comfort in her words. I let them override my loneliness, and listen to her tell the whole story:

Okay, so your dad and I are driving to Great America. We want to take your sister Sammy there for the day. As soon as I got up in the morning I felt a stabbing pain. I doubled over and could barely walk. Your dad took me to the hospital. The nurses asked me if there was a chance that I was pregnant, and I said I didn't think so. But, sure enough, I took a pregnancy test and learned I was pregnant. Then I had an ultrasound.

They told me I had an ectopic pregnancy, meaning you were in a fallopian tube and not in the uterus where you were supposed to be. They told me that I was going to have to have an emergency D&C.

Of course, I was devastated. I called up my good friend Rose and asked her to come to the hospital and pray with me. She came, and we prayed in the bathroom together. We asked God to move the baby into my uterus. Immediately, the pain stopped.

But the doctors were not so convinced. They said I could hemorrhage internally. All I wanted to do was go home.

Then the doctor, who was very irritated with me, said, "Fine, you want a second opinion? I'll get you a second opinion." We waited for another doctor to come, Dr. Thompson. He finally came, and both doctors kept referring to you as a "mass", never once calling you a child or a baby.

But they did another test and were astounded. "Oh my God," Dr. Thompson said. "You're not going to believe this, but your baby is in the uterus!"

Even with you in my uterus, I still had a 50/50 chance of carrying you to term.

But I knew you were going to be just fine!

So, one morning, I'm lying on the couch. I had to keep pushing your ass over because you were always leaning on my bladder. Suddenly, I hear a loud noise, like the sound of a pop of champagne. My water broke!

Your dad wakes up, and he calmly starts making coffee, taking his time. He had been through this before with your sister Sammy. He knew we had a little time.

I was in labor for almost ten hours. Back labor! I was begging for pain meds, but they wouldn't give me any more. I was stuck in transition for two and a half hours. I thought you were going to be this huge baby. It was all water! You were a tiny little thing. Five pounds and fifteen ounces. Just gorgeous.

I'm a little person who feels big things and enjoys laughing at and identifying with stories like this. Like so many people at the moment, I feel the momentum of mass healing. Thirty is my year to heal.

Who among us are modern-day spiritual leaders? And I'm not talking about the leaders of megachurches with a set of glistening wolf teeth and pockets full of cash. I know *they're* out there; *we're* actually everywhere, moving and loving, existing outside dogma.

The God I've created in my own heart doesn't want to control me through fear, fire, and a lineage of rightful heirs. She doesn't want me to spend my whole life repenting. She does want me to be happy and pull those little gifts from the inside of my body and use them in the only ways I know how to.

Maybe we have the same God, maybe they just appear in different contexts. You don't owe me anything. You don't have to worry about where my soul goes when I'm dead. I just hope you care about working on yourself and your potential versus trying to break down others. That's what the God of every faith would want.

Maya and I settle for a walk behind my apartment complex. I shove her barrel of a body into a sweater she's outgrown. Power lines buzz over my head. My mom used to be afraid these things would give us cancer. I shiver underneath them and toss a stick that Maya offers up to me. When she shits, I pick it up with a thin transparent bag, and walk it over to the trash can. I pick up three pieces of trash and deposit them into the same can.

The world isn't mine to save or conquer, but I still aim to do what I can when it's presented to me. And I want to find love, too, you know?

Previously published

Whoopie Pie, Echolocation: *Bird's Thumb*

Shades of Nude: *Bayou Magazine*

Crap Apples: *Better Than Starbucks*

Lenny: *Jersey Devil Press*

Acknowledgements

Thank you to the best writer I know and my soul seahorse, Alexa. Thank you for believing in me, for getting lost and found on camping trips with me, and for saying the hard things. Here's to my friend, Jess, for all the poems, meals, and bird analogies you've shared. Thank you to my editor, Ruth, for spending so much time getting to know these stories. A big thank you to every single English teacher I've ever had for showing me the healing power of words. Thank you, Mom, for teaching me that dancing is one of the best cures for sadness.

Made in the USA
Middletown, DE
29 June 2023